POLITICALLY CORRECT
THE ULTIMATE STORYBOOK

Politically Correct Bedtime Stories
Once Upon a More Enlightened Time
Politically Correct Holiday Stories

POLITICALLY CORRECT
THE ULTIMATE STORYBOOK

Politically Correct Bedtime Stories
Once Upon a More Enlightened Time
Politically Correct Holiday Stories

JAMES FINN GARNER

SMITHMARK

This edition contains the complete and unabridged texts of the original editions.

This omnibus was originally published in separate volumes under the original titles:

Politically Correct Bedtime Stories copyright © 1994 by James Finn Garner,
published by Macmillan Books USA, a division of Simon & Schuster
Once Upon a More Enlightened Time copyright © 1995 by James Finn Garner,
published by Macmillan Books USA, a division of Simon & Schuster
Politically Correct Holiday Stories copyright © 1995 by James Finn Garner,
published by Macmillan Books USA, a division of Simon & Schuster

This edition published in 1998 by
SMITHMARK Publishers
a division of U.S. Media Holdings, Inc.
115 West 18th Street
New York, NY 10011

SMITHMARK Books are available for bulk purchase for sales promotion
and premium use. For details write or call the manager of special sales,
SMITHMARK Publishers, 115 West 18th Street, New York, NY 10011.

Library of Congress Cataloging-In-Publication Data Is Available

ISBN: 0-7651-0867-4

Printed in the United States of America

10 9 8 7 6 5 4 3 2

CONTENTS

ONCE UPON A MORE ENLIGHTENED TIME   95

POLITICALLY CORRECT HOLIDAY STORIES   **187**

POLITICALLY CORRECT
BEDTIME STORIES

To the Theater of the Bizarre,
including Pepe, Armando, Egon, Ted,
Matteo, Nick, and Julietta; James Ghelkins, Jr.,
and Willie, Smitty, and Jocko
of the Teamsters Children's Puppet Theater;
and Others too numerous to mention.
To Carol, for help and encouragement,
and to Lies, for everything.

INTRODUCTION

When they were first written, the stories on which the following tales are based certainly served their purpose—to entrench the patriarchy, to estrange people from their own natural impulses, to demonize "evil" and to "reward" an "objective" "good." However much we might like to, we cannot blame the Brothers Grimm for their insensitivity to womyn's issues, minority cultures, and the environment. Likewise, in the self-righteous Copenhagen of Hans Christian Andersen, the inalienable rights of mermaids were hardly given a second thought.

Today, we have the opportunity—and the obligation—to rethink these "classic" stories so they reflect more enlightened times. To that effort I submit this humble book. While its original title, *Fairy Stories For a Modern World*, was abandoned for obvious reasons (kudos to my editor for pointing out my heterosexualist bias), I think the collection stands on its own. This, however, is just a start. Certain stories, such as "The Duckling That Was Judged on Its Personal Merits and Not on Its Physical Appearance," were deleted for space reasons. I expect I have volumes left in me, and I hope this book sparks the righteous imaginations of other writers and, of course, leaves an indelible mark on our children.

If, through omission or commission, I have inadvertently displayed any sexist, racist, culturalist, nationalist, regionalist, ageist, lookist, ableist, sizeist, speciesist, intellectualist, socioeconomicist, ethnocentrist, phallocentrist, heteropatriarchalist, or other type of bias as yet unnamed, I apologize and encourage your suggestions for rectification. In the quest to develop meaningful literature that is totally free from bias and purged from the influences of its flawed cultural past, I doubtless have made some mistakes.

LITTLE RED RIDING HOOD

here once was a young person named Red Riding Hood who lived with her mother on the edge of a large wood. One day her mother asked her to take a basket of fresh fruit and mineral water to her grandmother's house—not because this was womyn's work, mind you, but because the deed was generous and helped engender a feeling of community. Furthermore, her grandmother was *not* sick, but rather was in full physical and mental health and was fully capable of taking care of herself as a mature adult.

So Red Riding Hood set off with her basket through the woods. Many people believed that the forest was a foreboding and dangerous place and never set foot in it. Red Riding Hood, however, was confident enough in her own budding sexuality that such obvious Freudian imagery did not intimidate her.

On the way to Grandma's house, Red Riding Hood was accosted by a wolf, who asked her what was in her basket. She replied, "Some healthful snacks for my grandmother, who is certainly capable of taking care of herself as a mature adult."

The wolf said, "You know, my dear, it isn't safe for a little girl to walk through these woods alone."

Red Riding Hood said, "I find your sexist remark offensive in the extreme, but I will ignore it because of your traditional status as an outcast from society, the stress of which has caused you to develop your own, entirely valid, worldview. Now, if you'll excuse me, I must be on my way."

Red Riding Hood walked on along the main path. But, because his status outside society had freed him from slavish adherence to linear, Western-style thought, the wolf knew a quicker route to Grandma's house. He burst into the house and ate Grandma, an entirely valid course of action for a carnivore such as himself. Then, unhampered by rigid, traditionalist notions of what was masculine or feminine, he put on Grandma's nightclothes and crawled into bed.

Red Riding Hood entered the cottage and said, "Grandma, I have brought you some fat-free, sodium-free snacks to salute you in your role of a wise and nurturing matriarch."

From the bed, the wolf said softly, "Come closer, child, so that I might see you."

Red Riding Hood said, "Oh, I forgot you are as optically challenged as a bat. Grandma, what big eyes you have!"

"They have seen much, and forgiven much, my dear."

"Grandma, what a big nose you have—only relatively, of course, and certainly attractive in its own way."

"It has smelled much, and forgiven much, my dear."

"Grandma, what big teeth you have!"

The wolf said, "I am happy with *who* I am and *what* I am," and leaped out of bed. He grabbed Red Riding Hood in his claws, intent on devouring her. Red Riding Hood screamed, not out of alarm at the wolf's apparent tendency toward cross-dressing, but because of his willful invasion of her personal space.

Her screams were heard by a passing woodchopper-person (or log-fuel technician, as he preferred to be called). When he burst into the cottage, he saw the melee and tried to intervene. But as he raised his ax, Red Riding Hood and the wolf both stopped.

"And just what do you think you're doing?" asked Red Riding Hood.

The woodchopper-person blinked and tried to answer, but no words came to him.

"Bursting in here like a Neanderthal, trusting your weapon to do your thinking for you!" she exclaimed. "Sexist! Speciesist! How dare you assume that womyn and wolves can't solve their own problems without a man's help!"

When she heard Red Riding Hood's impassioned speech, Grandma jumped out of the wolf's mouth, seized the woodchopper-person's ax, and cut his head off. After this ordeal, Red Riding Hood, Grandma, and the wolf felt a certain commonality of purpose. They decided to set up an alternative household based on mutual respect and cooperation, and they lived together in the woods happily ever after.

THE EMPEROR'S
NEW CLOTHES

ar away, in a time long past, there lived a traveling tailor who found himself in an unfamiliar country. Now, tailors who move from place to place normally keep to themselves and are careful not to overstep the bounds of local decency. This tailor, though, was overly gregarious and decorum-impaired, and soon he was at a local inn, abusing alcohol, invading the personal space of the female employees, and telling unenlightened stories about tinkers, dung-gatherers, and other tradespeople.

The innkeeper complained to the police, who

grabbed the tailor and dragged him in front of the emperor. As you might expect, a lifetime of belief in the absolute legitimacy of the monarchy and in the inherent superiority of males had turned the emperor into a vain and wisdom-challenged tyrant. The tailor noticed these traits and decided to use them to his advantage.

The emperor asked, "Do you have any last request before I banish you from my domain forever?"

The tailor replied, "Only that your majesty allow me the honor of crafting a new royal wardrobe. For I have brought with me a special fabric that is so rare and fine that it can be seen only by certain people— the type of people you'd want to have in *your* realm—people who are politically correct, morally righteous, intellectually astute, culturally tolerant, and who don't smoke, drink, laugh at sexist jokes, watch too much television, listen to country music, or barbecue."

After a moment's thought, the emperor agreed to this request. He was flattered by the fascist and testosterone-heavy idea that the empire and its inhabitants existed only to make him look good. It would be like having a trophy wife and multiplying that feeling by 100,000.

Of course, no such rarefied fabric existed. Years of living outside the bounds of normal society had forced the tailor to develop his own moral code that obliged him to swindle and embarrass the emperor in the name of independent craftspeople everywhere. So, as he diligently labored, he was able to convince the emperor that he was cutting and sewing pieces of fabric that, in the strictest objective sense of reality, didn't exist.

When the tailor announced that he was finished, the emperor looked at his new robes in the mirror. As he stood there, naked as the day he was born, one could see how years of exploiting the peasantry had turned his body into an ugly mass of puffy white flesh. The emperor, of course, saw this too, but pretended that he could see the beautiful, politically correct robes. To show off his new splendor, he ordered a parade to be held the next day.

On the following morning, his subjects lined the streets for the big parade. Word had spread about the emperor's new clothes that only enlightened people with healthy lifestyles could see, and everyone was determined to be more right-minded than his or her neighbor.

The parade began with great hoopla. As the

emperor marched his pale, bloated, patriarchal carcass down the street, everyone loudly oohed and ahed at his beautiful new clothes. All except one small boy, who shouted:

"The emperor is naked!"

The parade stopped. The emperor paused. A hush fell over the crowd, until one quick-thinking peasant shouted:

"No, he isn't. The emperor is merely endorsing a clothing-optional lifestyle!"

A cheer went up from the crowd, and the throngs stripped off their clothes and danced in the sun, as Nature had intended. The country was clothing-optional from that day forward, and the tailor, deprived of any livelihood, packed up his needle and thread and was never heard from again.

THE THREE
LITTLE PIGS

nce there were three little pigs who lived together in mutual respect and in harmony with their environment. Using materials that were indigenous to the area, they each built a beautiful house. One pig built a house of straw, one a house of sticks, and one a house of dung, clay, and creeper vines shaped into bricks and baked in a small kiln. When they were finished, the pigs were satisfied with their work and settled back to live in peace and self-determination.

But their idyll was soon shattered. One day, along came a big, bad wolf with expansionist ideas. He saw the pigs and grew very hungry, in both a physical and an ideological sense. When the pigs saw the wolf, they ran into the house of straw. The wolf ran up to the house and banged on the door, shouting, "Little pigs, little pigs, let me in!"

The pigs shouted back, "Your gunboat tactics hold no fear for pigs defending their homes and culture."

But the wolf wasn't to be denied what he thought was his manifest destiny. So he huffed and puffed and blew down the house of straw. The frightened pigs ran to the house of sticks, with the wolf in hot pursuit. Where the house of straw had stood, other wolves bought up the land and started a banana plantation.

At the house of sticks, the wolf again banged on the door and shouted, "Little pigs, little pigs, let me in!"

The pigs shouted back, "Go to hell, you carnivorous, imperialistic oppressor!"

At this, the wolf chuckled condescendingly. He thought to himself: "They are so childlike in their ways. It will be a shame to see them go, but progress cannot be stopped."

So the wolf huffed and puffed and blew down the house of sticks. The pigs ran to the house of bricks, with the wolf close at their heels. Where the house of sticks had stood, other wolves built a time-share condo resort complex for vacationing wolves, with each unit a fiberglass reconstruction of the house of sticks, as well as native curio shops, snorkeling, and dolphin shows.

At the house of bricks, the wolf again banged on the door and shouted, "Little pigs, little pigs, let me in!"

This time in response, the pigs sang songs of solidarity and wrote letters of protest to the United Nations.

By now the wolf was getting angry at the pigs' refusal to see the situation from the carnivore's point of view. So he huffed and puffed, and huffed and puffed, then grabbed his chest and fell over dead from a massive heart attack brought on from eating too many fatty foods.

The three little pigs rejoiced that justice had triumphed and did a little dance around the corpse of the wolf. Their next step was to liberate their homeland. They gathered together a band of other pigs who had been forced off their lands. This new brigade of *porcinistas* attacked the resort complex with machine guns and rocket launchers and slaughtered the cruel wolf oppressors, sending a clear signal to the rest of the hemisphere not to meddle in their internal affairs. Then the pigs set up a model social-ist democracy with free education, universal health care, and affordable housing for everyone.

Please note: The wolf in this story was a metaphorical con-struct. No actual wolves were harmed in the writing of the story.

RUMPELSTILTSKIN

ong ago in a kingdom far away, there lived a miller who was very economically disadvantaged. This miller shared his humble dwelling with his only daughter, an independent young wommon named Esmeralda. Now, the miller was very ashamed of his poverty, rather than angry at the economic system that had marginalized him, and was always searching for a way to get rich quick.

"If only I could get my daughter to marry a rich man," he mused, in a sexist and archaic way, "she'll be fulfilled and I'll never have to work another day in my life." To this shabby end, he had an inspiration. He would start a rumor that his daughter was able to spin common barnyard straw into pure gold. With this untruth, he would be able to attract the attention of many rich men and marry off Esmeralda.

The rumor spread through the kingdom in a manner that just happened to be like wildfire and soon reached the prince. As greedy and gullible as most men of his station, he believed the rumor and invited Esmeralda to his castle for a May Day festival. But when she arrived, he had her thrown into a dungeon filled with straw and ordered her to spin it into gold.

Locked in the dungeon, fearing for her life, Esmeralda sat on the floor and wept. Never had the exploitativeness of the patriarchy been made so apparent to her. As she cried, a diminutive man in a funny hat appeared in the dungeon.

"Why are you crying, my dear?" he asked.

Esmeralda was startled but answered him: "The prince has ordered me to spin all this straw into gold."

"But why are you crying?" he asked again.

"Because it can't be *done*. What are you, specially abled or something?"

The differently statured man laughed and said, "Dearie, you are thinking too much with the left side of your brain, you are. But you are in luck. I will show you how to perform this task, yes, but first you must promise to give me what I want in return."

With no alternative, Esmeralda gave her assent. To turn the straw into gold, they took it to a nearby farmers' cooperative, where it was used to thatch an old roof. With a drier home, the farmers became healthier and more productive, and they brought forth a record harvest of wheat for local consumption. The children of the kingdom grew strong and tall, went to a cooperative school, and gradually turned the kingdom into a model democracy with no economic or sexual injustice and low infant mortality rates. For his part, the prince was captured by an angry mob and stabbed to death with pitchforks outside the palace. As new investment money poured in from all over the world, the farmers remembered Esmeralda's generous gift of straw and rewarded her with numerous chests of gold.

When all this was done, the diminutive man in the funny hat laughed and said, *"That* is how you turn straw into gold." Then his expression became menacing. "Now that I have done my work, you must fulfill your part of the bargain. You must give me your first-born child!"

Esmeralda shot back at him, "I don't have to negotiate with anyone who would interfere with my reproductive rights!"

The vertically challenged man was taken aback by the conviction in her voice. Deciding on a change in tactics, he said slyly, "Fair enough, dearie. I'll let you out of the bargain if you can guess what my name is."

"All right," said Esmeralda. She paused a second, tapped her chin with her finger, and said, "Would your name be . . . oh, I don't know, maybe . . . Rumpelstiltskin?"

"AAAAAKKKK!!" shrieked the man of nonstandard height. "But . . . but . . . how did you know?"

She replied, "You are still wearing your name badge from the Little People's Empowerment Seminar."

Rumpelstiltskin screamed in anger and stamped his foot, at which point the earth cracked open and swallowed him up in a rush of smoke and sulphur. With her gold, Esmeralda moved to California to open a birth-control clinic, where she showed other womyn how not to be enslaved by their reproductive systems and lived to the end of her days as a fulfilled, dedicated single person.

THE THREE CODEPENDENT GOATS GRUFF

nce on a lovely mountainside lived three goats who were related as siblings. Their name was Gruff, and they were a very close family. During the winter months they lived in a lush, green valley, eating grass and doing other things in a naturally goatish manner. When summer came, they would travel up the mountainside to where the pasture was sweeter. This way, they did not overgraze their valley and kept their ecological footprint as small as possible.

To get to this pasture, the goats had to cross a bridge over a wide chasm. When the first days of summer came, one goat set out to cross the bridge. This goat was the least chronologically accomplished of the siblings and thus had achieved the least superiority in size. When he reached the bridge, he lashed on his safety helmet and grasped the handrail. But as he began to cross, a menacing growl came from beneath the bridge.

Over the railing and onto the bridge leaped a troll—hairy, dirt-accomplished, and odor-enhanced. "Yaaarrrgh!!" intoned the troll. "I am the keeper of this bridge, and while goats may have the right to cross it, I'll eat any that try!"

"But why, Mr. Troll?" bleated the goat.

"Because I'm a troll, and proud of it. I have a troll's needs, and those needs include eating goats, so you better respect them or else."

The goat was frightened. "Certainly, sir," he stammered. "If eating me would help you become a more complete troll, nothing would please me more. But I really can't commit to that course of action without first consulting my siblings. Will you excuse me?" And the goat ran back to the valley.

Next, the middle sibling goat came up to the

bridge. This goat was more chronologically advanced than the first goat and so enjoyed an advantage in size (although this did not make him a better or more deserving goat). He was about to cross the bridge when the troll stopped him.

"Nature has made me a troll," he said, "and I embrace my trollhood. Would you deny me my right to live the life of a troll as fully and effectively as I can?"

"Me? Never!" exclaimed the goat proudly.

"Then stand still there while I come over and eat you up. And don't try to run away; I would take that as a personal affront." He began to invade the goat's caprinal space.

"However," blurted the goat, "I have a very close family, and it would be selfish of me to allow myself to be eaten without asking their opinion. I have respect for their feelings, too. I would hate to think that my absence would cause them any emotional stress, if I hadn't first. . . ."

"*Go* then!" screamed the troll.

"I'll rush back here as soon as we reach a consensus," the goat said, "for it's not fair to keep you in suspense."

"You're too kind," sighed the troll, and the goat ran back to the valley. As his hunger grew, the troll began to feel a real grievance toward the goats. If he didn't get to eat at least one of them, he was determined to go to the authorities.

When the third goat came to the bridge, the troll discovered that he was nearly twice the troll's size, with large, sharp horns and hard, heavy hooves. The troll felt his physical-intimidation prerogative fading fast. As fear turned his insides into jelly, the troll sank to his knees and pleaded, "Oh, please, please forgive me! I was using you and your goat siblings for my own selfish ends. I don't know what drove me to it, but I've seen the error of my ways."

The goat, too, got down on what passed for knees in goats and said, "Now, now, you can't take all the blame for yourself. Our presence and supreme edibility put you in this situation. My siblings and I all feel terrible. Please, *you* must forgive *us.*"

The troll began to sob. "No, no, it's all my fault. I threatened and bullied you all, just for the sake of my own survival. How selfish I was!"

But the goat would have none of this. "We were the selfish ones. We only wanted to save our own skins, and we totally neglected your needs. Please, eat me now!"

"No," the troll said, "you must butt me off this bridge for my insensitivity and selfishness."

"I'll do no such thing," said the goat, "since we all tempted you in the first place. Here, have a chomp. Go ahead."

"I'm telling you," the troll insisted, standing up, "I'm the guilty one here. Now, knock me off this bridge and be quick about it!"

"Look," said the goat, rearing to his full height, "no one is going to take away my blame for this, not even you, so eat me before I pop you in the nose."

"Don't play guiltier-than-thou with me, Hornhead!"

"'Hornhead'? You smelly hairball! I'll show you guilt!" And with that, they wrestled and bit and punched and kicked as each sought to don the mantle of blame.

The other two goats bounded up to the bridge and sized up the fight. Feeling guilty at not accepting enough of the blame, they joined the others in a whirling ball of hair, hooves, horns, and teeth. But the little bridge was not built to carry such weight. It shook and swayed and finally buckled, hurling the troll and the three codependent goats Gruff into the chasm. On their way down, they each felt relieved that they would finally get what they deserved, plus, as a bonus, a little extra guilt for the fate of the others.

RAPUNZEL

here once lived an economically disadvantaged tinker and his wife. His lack of material accomplishment is not meant to imply that all tinkers are economically marginalized, or that if they are, they deserve to be so. While the archetype of the tinker is generally the whipping person in classical bedtime stories, this particular individual was a tinker by trade and just happened to be economically disadvantaged.

The tinker and his wife lived in a little hovel next to the modest estate of a local witch. From their window, they could see the witch's meticulously kept garden, a nauseating attempt to impose human notions of order onto Nature.

The wife of the tinker was pregnant, and as she gazed at the witch's garden, she began to crave some of the lettuce she saw growing there. She begged the tinker to jump the fence and get some for her. The tinker finally submitted, and at night he jumped the wall and liberated some of the lettuce. But before he could get back, the witch caught him.

Now, this witch was very kindness-impaired. (This is not meant to imply that all, or even some, witches are that way, nor to deny this particular witch her right to express whatever disposition came naturally to her. Far from it, her disposition was without doubt due to many factors of her upbringing and socialization, which, unfortunately, must be omitted here in the interest of brevity.)

As mentioned earlier, the witch was kindness-impaired, and the tinker was extremely frightened. She held him by the scruff of the neck and asked, "Where are you going with my lettuce?"

The tinker might have argued with her over the concept of ownership and stated that the lettuce rightfully "belonged" to anyone who was hungry and had nerve enough to take it. Instead, in a degrading spectacle, he pleaded for mercy. "It was my wife's fault," he cried in a characteristically male manner. "She is pregnant and has a craving for some of your lovely lettuce. Please spare me. Although a single-parent household is certainly acceptable, please don't kill me and deprive my child of a stable, two-parent family structure."

The witch thought for a moment, then let go of the tinker's neck and disappeared without a word. The tinker gratefully went home with the lettuce. A few months later, and after agonizing pain that a man will never really be able to appreciate, the tinker's wife gave birth to a beautiful, healthy prewommon. They named the baby Rapunzel, after a type of lettuce.

Not long after this, the witch appeared at their door, demanding that they give her the child in return for the witch's having spared the tinker's life in the garden. What could they do? Their powerless station in life had always left them open to exploitation, and this time they felt they had no alternative. They gave Rapunzel to the witch, who sped away.

The witch took the child deep into the woods and imprisoned her in a tall tower, the symbolism of which should be obvious. There Rapunzel grew to wommonhood. The tower had no door or stairs, but it did boast a single window at the top. The only way for anyone to get to the window was for Rapunzel to let down her long, luxurious hair and climb it to the top, the symbolism of which should also be obvious.

The witch was Rapunzel's only companion. She would stand at the foot of the tower and shout,

> "Rapunzel, Rapunzel, let down your hair,
> "That I might climb your golden stair."

Rapunzel obediently did as she was told. Thus for years she let her body be exploited for the transportational needs of another. The witch loved music and taught Rapunzel to sing. They passed many long hours singing together in the tower.

One day a young prince rode near the tower and heard Rapunzel singing. But as he rode closer to find the source of the lovely sound, he spied the witch and hid himself and his equine companion in the trees. He watched as the witch called out to Rapunzel, the hair fell down, and the witch climbed up. Again, he heard the beautiful singing. Later, when the witch finally exited the tower and disappeared in the other direction, the prince came out of the woods and called up:

"Rapunzel, Rapunzel, let down your hair,
"That I might climb your golden stair."

The hair cascaded from the window, and he climbed up.

When the prince saw Rapunzel, her greater-than-average physical attractiveness and her long, luxurious hair led him to think, in a typically lookist way, that her personality would also be beautiful. (This is not to imply that all princes judge people solely on their appearance, nor to deny this particular prince his right to make such assumptions. Please see the disclaimers in the paragraphs above.)

The prince said, "Oh, beautiful damsel, I heard you singing as I rode by on my horse. Please sing for me again."

Rapunzel didn't know what to make of this person, since she had never seen a man up close before. He seemed a strange creature—large, hairy in the face, and possessing a strong, musky odor. For reasons she could not explain, Rapunzel found this combination somewhat attractive and opened her mouth to sing.

"Stop right there!" screamed a voice from the window. The witch had returned!

"How . . . how did you get up here?" Rapunzel asked.

"I had an extra set of hair made, in case of emergency," said the witch matter-of-factly. "And this certainly looks like one. Listen to me, Prince! I built this tower to keep Rapunzel away from men like you. I taught her to sing, training her voice for years. She'll stay here and sing for no one but me, because I am the only one who truly loves her."

"We can talk about your codependency problems later," said the prince. "But first let me hear . . . Rapunzel, is it? . . . let me hear Rapunzel sing."

"NO!" screamed the witch. "I'm going to throw you from the tower into the thorn-of-color bushes below so that your eyes will be gouged out and you'll wander the countryside cursing your bad luck for the rest of your life!"

"You may want to reconsider that," said the prince. "I have some friends in the recording industry, you see, who would be very interested in . . . Rapunzel, wasn't it? Different, kind of catchy, I suppose. . . ."

"I knew it! You want to take her from me!"

"No, no, I want you to continue to train her, to nurture her . . . as her *manager,*" said the prince.

"Then, when the time is right, say a week or two, you can unleash her talent on the world and we can all rake in the cash."

The witch paused for a second to think about this, and her demeanor visibly softened. She and the prince began to discuss record contracts and video deals, as well as possible marketing ideas, including life-like Rapunzel™ dolls with their very own miniature stereo Tune-Towers™.

As Rapunzel watched, her suspicions turned into revulsion. For years, her hair had been exploited for the transportational needs of others. Now they wanted to exploit her voice as well. "So, rapaciousness does not depend solely on gender," she realized with a sigh.

Rapunzel edged her way to the window without being seen. She stepped out and climbed down the second set of hair to the prince's waiting horse. She dislodged the hair and took it with her as she rode off, leaving the witch and the prince to argue about royalties and percentages in their phallus-shaped tower.

Rapunzel rode to the city and rented a room in a building that had real stairs. She later established the non-profit Foundation for the Free Proliferation of

Music and cut off her hair for a fund-raising auction. She sang for free in coffee houses and art galleries for the rest of her days, always refusing to exploit for money other people's desires to hear her sing.

CINDERELLA

here once lived a young wommon named Cinderella, whose natural birthmother had died when Cinderella was but a child. A few years after, her father married a widow with two older daughters. Cinderella's mother-of-step treated her very cruelly, and her sisters-of-step made her work very hard, as if she were their own personal unpaid laborer.

One day an invitation arrived at their house. The prince was celebrating his exploitation of the dispossessed and marginalized peasantry by throwing a fancy dress ball. Cinderella's sisters-of-step were very excited to be invited to the palace. They began to plan the expensive clothes they would use to alter

45

and enslave their natural body images to emulate an unrealistic standard of feminine beauty. (It was especially unrealistic in their case, as they were differently visaged enough to stop a clock.) Her mother-of-step also planned to go to the ball, so Cinderella was working harder than a dog (an appropriate if unfortunately speciesist metaphor).

When the day of the ball arrived, Cinderella helped her mother- and sisters-of-step into their ball gowns. A formidable task: It was like trying to force ten pounds of processed nonhuman animal carcasses into a five-pound skin. Next came immense cosmetic augmentation, which it would be best not to describe at all. As evening fell, her mother- and sisters-of-step left Cinderella at home to finish her housework. Cinderella was sad, but she contented herself with her Holly Near records.

Suddenly there was a flash of light, and in front of Cinderella stood a man dressed in loose-fitting, all-cotton clothes and wearing a wide-brimmed hat. At first Cinderella thought he was a Southern lawyer or a bandleader, but he soon put her straight.

"Hello, Cinderella, I am your fairy godperson, or individual deity proxy, if you prefer. So, you want to go to the ball, eh? And bind yourself into the male concept of beauty? Squeeze into some tight-fitting dress that will cut off your circulation? Jam your feet into high-heeled shoes that will ruin your bone structure? Paint your face with chemicals and make-up that have been tested on nonhuman animals?"

"Oh yes, definitely," she said in an instant. Her fairy godperson heaved a great sigh and decided to put off her political education till another day. With his magic, he enveloped her in a beautiful, bright light and whisked her away to the palace.

Many, many carriages were lined up outside the palace that night; apparently, no one had ever thought of carpooling. Soon, in a heavy, gilded carriage painfully pulled by a team of horse-slaves, Cinderella arrived. She was dressed in a clinging gown woven of silk stolen from unsuspecting silkworms. Her hair was festooned with pearls plundered from hard-working, defenseless oysters. And on her feet, dangerous though it may seem, she wore slippers made of finely cut crystal.

Every head in the ballroom turned as Cinderella entered. The men stared at and lusted after this wommon who had captured perfectly their Barbie-doll ideas of feminine desirability. The womyn, trained at an early age to despise their own bodies, looked at Cinderella with envy and spite. Cinderella's own mother- and sisters-of-step, consumed with jealousy, failed to recognize her.

Cinderella soon caught the roving eye of the prince, who was busy discussing jousting and bear-baiting with his cronies. Upon seeing her, the prince was struck with a fit of not being able to speak as well as the majority of the population. "Here," he thought, "is a wommon that I could make my princess and impregnate with the progeny of our perfect genes, and thus make myself the envy of every other prince for miles around. And she's blond, too!"

The prince began to cross the ballroom toward his intended prey. His cronies also began to walk toward Cinderella. So did every other male in the ballroom who was younger than 70 and not serving drinks.

Cinderella was proud of the commotion she was causing. She walked with head high and carried herself like a wommon of eminent social standing. But soon it became clear that the commotion was turning into something ugly, or at least socially dysfunctional.

The prince had made it clear to his friends that he was intent on "possessing" the young wommon. But the prince's resoluteness angered his pals, for they too lusted after her and wanted to own her. The men began to shout and push each other. The prince's best friend, who was a large if cerebrally constrained duke, stopped him halfway across the dance floor and insisted that *he* was going to have Cinderella. The prince's response was a swift kick to the groin, which left the duke temporarily inactive. But the prince was quickly seized by other sex-crazed males, and he disappeared into a pile of human animals.

The womyn were appalled by this vicious display of testosterone, but try as they might, they were unable to separate the combatants. To the other womyn, it seemed that Cinderella was the cause of all the trouble, so they encircled her and began to display very unsisterly hostility. She tried to escape, but her impractical glass slippers made it nearly impossible. Fortunately for her, none of the other womyn were shod any better.

The noise grew so loud that no one heard the clock in the tower chime midnight. When the bell rang the twelfth time, Cinderella's beautiful gown and slippers disappeared, and she was dressed once again in her peasant's rags. Her mother- and sisters-of-step recognized her now, but kept quiet to avoid embarrassment.

The womyn grew silent at this magical transformation. Freed from the confinements of her gown and slippers, Cinderella sighed and stretched and scratched her ribs. She smiled, closed her eyes and said, "Kill me now if you want, sisters, but at least I'll die in comfort."

The womyn around her again grew envious, but this time they took a different approach: Instead of exacting vengeance on her, they stripped off their bodices, corsets, shoes, and every other confining garment. They danced and jumped and screeched in sheer joy, comfortable at last in their shifts and bare feet.

Had the men looked up from their macho dance of destruction, they would have seen many desirable womyn dressed as if for the boudoir. But they never ceased pounding, punching, kicking, and clawing each other until, to the last man, they were dead.

The womyn clucked their tongues but felt no remorse. The palace and realm were theirs now. Their first official act was to dress the men in their discarded dresses and tell the media that the fight arose when someone threatened to expose the cross-dressing tendencies of the prince and his cronies. Their second was to set up a clothing co-op that produced only comfortable, practical clothes for womyn. Then they hung a sign on the castle advertising CinderWear (for that was what the new clothing was called), and through self-determination and clever marketing, they all—even the mother- and sisters-of-step—lived happily ever after.

GOLDILOCKS

hrough the thicket, across the river, and deep, deep in the woods, lived a family of bears—a Papa Bear, a Mama Bear, and a Baby Bear—and they all lived together anthropomorphically in a little cottage as a nuclear family. They were very sorry about this, of course, since the nuclear family has traditionally served to enslave womyn, instill a self-righteous moralism in its members, and imprint rigid notions of heterosexualist roles onto the next generation. Nevertheless, they tried to be happy and took steps to avoid these pitfalls, such as naming their offspring the non-gender-specific "Baby."

One day, in their little anthropomorphic cottage,

they sat down to breakfast. Papa Bear had prepared big bowls of all-natural porridge for them to eat. But straight off the stove, the porridge was too thermally enhanced to eat. So they left their bowls to cool and took a walk to visit their animal neighbors.

After the bears left, a melanin-impoverished young wommon emerged from the bushes and crept up to the cottage. Her name was Goldilocks, and she had been watching the bears for days. She was, you see, a biologist who specialized in the study of anthropomorphic bears. At one time she had been a professor, but her aggressive, masculine approach to science—ripping off the thin veil of Nature, exposing its secrets, penetrating its essence, using it for her own selfish needs, and bragging about such violations in the letters columns of various magazines—had led to her dismissal.

The rogue biologist had been watching the cottage for some time. Her intent was to collar the bears with radio transmitters and then follow them in their migratory and other life patterns, with an utter disregard for their personal (or rather, animal) privacy. With scientific espionage the only thing in mind, Goldilocks broke into the bears' cottage. In the kitchen, she laced the bowls of porridge with a tranquilizing potion. Then, in the bedroom, she rigged snares beneath the pillows of each bed. Her plan was to drug the bears and, when they stumbled into their bedroom to take a nap, lash radio collars to their necks as their heads hit the pillows.

Goldilocks chortled and thought: "These bears will be my ticket to the top! I'll show those twerps at the university the kind of guts it takes to do *real* research!" She crouched in a corner of the bedroom and waited. And waited, and waited some more. But the bears took so long to come back from their walk that she fell asleep.

When the bears finally came home, they sat down to eat breakfast. Then they stopped.

Papa Bear asked, "Does your porridge smell . . . off, Mama?"

Mama Bear replied, "Yes, it does. Does yours smell off, Baby?"

Baby Bear said, "Yes, it does. It smells kind of chemical-y."

Suspicious, they rose from the table and went into the living room. Papa Bear sniffed. He asked, "Do you smell something else, Mama?"

Mama Bear replied, "Yes, I do. Do you smell something else, Baby?"

Baby Bear said, "Yes, I do. It smells musky and sweaty and not at all clean."

They moved into the bedroom with growing alarm. Papa Bear asked, "Do you see a snare and a radio collar under my pillow. Mama?"

Mama Bear replied, "Yes I do. Do you see a snare and a radio collar under my pillow, Baby?"

Baby Bear said, "Yes I do, and I see the human who put them there!"

Baby Bear pointed in the corner to where Goldilocks slept. The bears growled, and Goldilocks awoke with a start. She sprang up and tried to run, but Papa Bear caught her with a swing of his paw, and Mama Bear did the same. With Goldilocks now a mobility nonpossessor, Mama and Papa Bear set on her with fang and claw. They gobbled her up, and soon there was nothing left of the maverick biologist but a bit of yellow hair and a clipboard.

Baby Bear watched with astonishment. When they were done, Baby Bear asked, "Mama, Papa, what have you done? I thought we were vegetarians."

Papa Bear burped. "We are," he said, "but we're always ready to try new things. Flexibility is just one more benefit of being multicultural."

SNOW WHITE

nce there was a young princess who was not at all unpleasant to look at and had a temperament that many found to be more pleasant than most other people's. Her nickname was Snow White, indicative of the discriminatory notions of associating pleasant or attractive qualities with light, and unpleasant or unattractive qualities with darkness. Thus, at an early age, Snow White was an unwitting if fortunate target for this type of colorist thinking.

When Snow White was quite young, her mother was suddenly stricken ill, grew more advanced in nonhealth, and finally was rendered nonviable. Her father, the king, grieved for what can be considered a healthy period of time, then asked another wommon to be his queen. Snow White did her best to please her new mother-of-step, but a cold distance remained between them.

The queen's prized possession was a magic mirror that would answer truthfully any question asked it. Now, years of social conditioning in a male hierarchical dictatorship had left the queen very insecure about her own self-worth. Physical beauty was the one standard she cared about now, and she defined herself solely in regard to her personal appearance. So every morning the queen would ask her mirror:

> "Mirror, mirror, on the wall,
> "Who's the fairest one of all?"

Her mirror would answer:

> "For all it's worth, O my queen,
> "Your beauty is the fairest to be seen."

That dialogue went on regularly until once when the queen was having a bad hair day and was desperately in need of support, she asked the usual question and the mirror answered:

"Alas, if worth be based on beauty,
"Snow White has surpassed you, cutie."

At this the queen flew into a rage. The chance to
work with Snow White to form a strong bond of sisterhood had long passed. Instead, the queen
indulged in an adopted masculine power trip and
ordered the royal woodsperson to take Snow White
into the forest and kill her. And, possibly to impress
the males in the royal court, she barbarously ordered
that the girl's heart be cut out and brought back to
her.

The woodsperson sadly agreed to these orders,
and led the girl, who was now actually a young
wommon, into the middle of the forest. But his connections to the earth and seasons had made him a
kind soul, and he couldn't bear to harm the girl. He
told Snow White of the oppressive and unsisterly
order of the queen and told her to run as deeply as
she could into the forest.

The frightened Snow White did as she was told.
The woodsperson, fearing the queen's wrath but
unwilling to take another life merely to indulge her
vanity, went into town and had the candy maker
concoct a heart of red marzipan. When he presented

this to the queen, she hungrily devoured the heart in a sickening display of pseudo-cannibalism.

Meanwhile, Snow White ran deep into the woods. Just when she thought she had fled as far as she could from civilization and its unhealthy influences, she stumbled upon a cottage. Inside she saw seven tiny beds, set in a row and all unmade. She also saw seven sets of dishes piled high in the sink and seven Barcaloungers in front of seven remote-controlled TVs. She surmised that the cottage belonged to either seven little men or one sloppy numerologist. The beds looked so inviting that the tired youngster curled up on one and immediately fell asleep.

When she awoke several hours later, she saw the faces of seven bearded, vertically challenged men surrounding the bed. She sat up with a start and gasped. One of the men said, "You see that? Just like a flighty woman: resting peacefully one minute, up and screaming the next."

"I agree," said another. "She'll disrupt our strong bond of brotherhood and create competition among us for her affections. I say we throw her in the river in a sack full of rocks."

"I agree we should get rid of her," said a third, "but why degrade the ecology? Let's just feed her to a bear or something and let her become part of the food chain."

"Hear, hear!"

"Sound thinking, brother."

When Snow White finally regained her senses, she begged, "Please, please don't kill me. I meant no harm by sleeping on your bed. I thought no one would ever notice."

"Ah, you see?" said one of the men. "Female preoccupations are already surfacing. She's complaining that we don't make our beds."

"Kill her! Kill her!"

"Please, no!" she cried. "I have traveled so deep into these woods because my mother-of-step, the queen, ordered me killed."

"See that? Internecine female vindictiveness!"

"Don't try and play the victim with *us*, kid!"

"QUIET!" boomed one of the men, who had flaming red hair and a nonhuman animal skin on his head. Snow White quickly realized that he was their leader and that her fate rested in his hands. "Explain yourself. What's your name, and why have you really come here?"

"My name is Snow White," she began, "and I've already told you: My mother-of-step, the queen, ordered a woodsperson to take me in the forest and kill me, but he took pity and told me to run away into the woods as far as I could."

"Just like a woman," grumbled one of the men under his breath, "get a man to do her dirty work."

The leader held up his hands for silence. He said, "Well, Snow White, if that's your story, I guess we'll have to believe you."

Snow White was beginning to resent her treatment but tried not to let it show. "And who are you guys, anyway?"

"We are known as the Seven Towering Giants," said the leader. Snow White's suppression of a giggle did not go unnoticed. The leader continued. "We are towering in *spirit* and so are *giants* among the men of the forest. We used to earn our living by digging in our mines, but we decided that such a rape of the planet was immoral and short-sighted (besides, the bottom fell out of the metals market). So now we are dedicated stewards of the earth and live here in harmony with nature. To make ends meet, we also conduct retreats for men who need to get in touch with their primitive masculine identities."

"So what does that involve," asked Snow White, "aside from drinking milk straight from the carton?"

"Your sarcasm is ill-advised," warned the leader of the Seven Towering Giants. "My fellow giants want to get rid of your corrupting feminine presence, and I might not be able to stop them, understand? My men, we must speak our hearts openly and honestly. Let us adjourn to the sweat lodge!"

The seven little men scampered out the front door, whooping and stripping off their clothes. Snow White didn't know what to do while waiting. For fear of stepping on anything that might be scurrying about amid the debris on the floor, she stayed on the bed, although she did manage to make it without ever stepping off.

Snow White heard drumming and shouts, and, soon after, the Seven Towering Giants came back into the cottage. They didn't smell as bad as she thought they would, and thankfully they all wore loincloths.

"Agggh! Look what she's done to my bed! I want her out of here! I want to change my vote!"

"Calm down, brother," said the leader. "Don't you see? This is just what we were talking about: contrasts. We can better measure our progress as true men if there is a female around for comparison."

The men grumbled among themselves about the

wisdom of this decision. But Snow White had had enough. "I resent being kept around like an object, just a yardstick for your egos and penises!"

"Fair enough," the leader said. "You're free to make your way back through the woods. Give our regards to the queen."

"Well, I guess I can stay until I figure out a new plan," she said.

"Very well," said the leader, "but we have a few ground rules. No dusting. No straightening up. And no rinsing out underwear in the sink."

"And no peeking in the sweat lodge."

"And stay away from our drums."

Meanwhile, back at the castle, the queen rejoiced at the thought that her rival in beauty had been eliminated. She puttered around her boudoir reading *Glamour* and *Elle*, and indulged herself with three whole pieces of chocolate without purging. Later, she confidently strolled up to her magic mirror and asked her same, sad question:

> "Mirror, mirror, on the wall,
> "Who's the fairest one of all?"

The mirror replied,

"Your weight is perfect for your shape and height,
"But for sheer OOOOMPH!, you can't beat Snow
  White."

At this news, the queen clenched her fists and screamed at the top of her lungs. For years, her insecurities had been eating away at her until now they turned her into someone who was morally out of the mainstream. With cunning and malice, she began to devise a plan to ensure the nonviability of her daughter-of-step.

A few days later, Snow White, to be sure she didn't touch or rearrange anything, was meditating on the floor in the middle of the cottage. Suddenly there was a knock on the door. Snow White opened the door to find a chronologically gifted woman with a basket in her hand. By the look of her clothes, she was apparently unfettered by the confines of regular employment.

"Help a woman of unreliable income, dearie," she said, "and buy one of my apples."

Snow White thought for a moment. In protest against agribusiness conglomerates, she had a personal rule against buying food from middlepersons. But her heart went out to the economically marginalized woman, so she said yes. What Snow White didn't know was that this was really the queen in disguise and that the apple had been chemically and genetically altered so that whoever bit it would sleep forever.

When Snow White handed over the money for the apple, you would have expected the queen to be gleeful that her plan for revenge was working. Instead, as she looked at Snow White's fine complexion and slim, taut body, she felt alternating waves of envy and self-revulsion. Finally, she burst into tears.

"Why, whatever is the matter?" asked Snow White.

"You're so young and beautiful," sobbed the disguised queen, "and I'm horrible to look at and getting worse."

"You shouldn't say that. After all, beauty comes from inside a person."

"I've been telling myself that for years," said the queen, "and I still don't believe it. How do you stay in such perfect shape?"

"Well, I meditate, work out in step aerobics three hours a day, and eat only half-portions of anything placed in front of me. Would you like me to show you?"

"Oh, yes, yes, please," said the queen. So they started out with 30 minutes of simple hatha yoga meditation, then worked out on the step for another hour. As they relaxed afterward, Snow White cut her apple in half and gave a piece to the queen. Without thinking, the queen bit into it, and both of them fell into a deep sleep.

Later that day, the Seven Towering Giants returned from a retreat in the woods, elaborately decked out in animal skins, feathers, and mud. With them was a prince from a nearby kingdom, who had come on this male retreat to find a cure for his impotence (or, as he preferred to call it, his involuntary suspension from phallocentric activity). They were all laughing and high-fiving until they saw the bodies and stopped short.

"What has happened?" asked the prince.

"Apparently our house guest and this other woman got into some sort of catfight and killed each other," surmised one giant.

"If they thought that by doing this, they could make us slaves to our weaker emotions, they're wrong," fumed another.

"Well, as long as we have to dispose of them, let's practice one of those Viking funerals we've read about."

"You know," said the prince, "this might sound a little sick, but I trust you guys. I find that younger one attractive. Extremely attractive. Would you fellows mind . . . um . . . waiting outside while I . . . ?"

"Stop right there!" said the leader of the giants. "Those half-eaten apple pieces, that filthy costume— this has all the earmarks of some sort of magic spell. They're not really dead at all."

"Whew," sighed the prince, "that makes me feel better. So, could you guys take five and let me . . . ?"

"Hold it, Prince," said the leader. "Does Snow White make you feel like a *man* again?"

"She certainly does. Now, could you guys . . . ?"

"Don't touch her! You'll break the spell." The leader thought for a minute and said, "My brothers, I see certain economic possibilities arising from this. If we kept Snow White around here in this state, we could advertise our retreats as impotency therapy."

The giants nodded in agreement with this idea, but the prince interrupted, "But what about me? I've already paid for my retreat. Why don't I get to, um, take the cure?"

"No dice, Prince," said the leader. "You can look but don't touch. Otherwise you'll break the spell. Tell you what, though. You can have the other one if you want."

"I don't want to sound classist," said the prince, "but she's not high enough *caliber* for me."

"That's pretty big talk from a man shooting blanks," said one of the giants, and everybody but the prince laughed.

The leader said, "Come on, brothers, let's lift these two off the floor and decide how we can best display them." It took three giants for each female, but they managed to get both bodies aloft. As soon as they did, however, the pieces of poisoned apple fell from the mouths of Snow White and the queen, and they awoke from the spell.

"What do you think you're doing? Put us down!" they shouted. The giants were so startled they almost dropped the womyn to the floor.

"That was the most sickening thing I have ever heard!" shouted the queen. "Offering us around like pieces of property!"

"And *you*," said Snow White to the prince, "trying to make it with a girl in a coma! Yuck!"

"Hey, don't blame me," said the prince. "It's a medical condition."

The leader of the giants said, "Don't start tossing blame around. You both broke into our property in the first place. I can call the police!"

"Don't try it, Napoleon," said the queen. "This forest is property of the crown. *You* are the ones who are trespassing!"

This rejoinder caused quite a stir, but not as big a commotion as when the queen warned: "And another thing. While we were immobile and you all blathered on in your sexist way, I had a personal awakening. From now on, I am going to dedicate my life to healing the rift between womyn's souls and their bodies. I am going to teach womyn to accept their natural body images and become whole again. Snow White and I are going to build a womyn's spa and conference center on this very spot, where we can hold retreats, caucuses, and ovariums for the sisters of the world."

There was much shouting and name-calling, but the queen eventually had her way. Before the Seven Towering Giants could be evicted from their home, though, they packed up their sweat lodge and moved deeper into the woods. The prince stayed on at the spa as a cute but harmless tennis pro. And Snow White and the queen became good friends and earned world-wide fame for their contributions to sisterhood. The giants were never heard from again, save for little muddy footprints that were sometimes found in the morning outside the windows of the spa's locker room.

CHICKEN LITTLE

hicken Little lived on a winding country lane surrounded by tall oak trees. (It should be mentioned here that the name "Little" was a family name, and not a derogatory, size-biased nickname. It was only by sheer coincidence that Chicken Little was also of shorter-than-average height.)

One day, Chicken Little was playing in the road when a gust of wind blew through the trees. An acorn was blown loose and hit Chicken Little squarely on the head.

Now, while Chicken Little had a small brain in the physical sense, she did use it to the best of her abilities. So when she screamed, "The sky is falling, the sky is falling!" her conclusion was not wrong or stupid or silly, only logically underenhanced.

Chicken Little ran down the road until she came to the house of her neighbor, Henny Penny, who was tending her garden. This was a simple task, since she didn't use any insecticide, herbicide, or fertilizer, and also permitted the native nonedible varieties of wildflower (sometimes branded "weeds") to mingle with her food crops. So, lost amid the foliage, Henny Penny heard Chicken Little's voice long before she saw her.

"The sky is falling! The sky is falling!"

Henny Penny stuck her head out from her garden and said, "Chicken Little! Why are you carrying on so?"

Chicken Little said, "I was playing in the road when a huge chunk of the sky fell and landed on my head. See? Here's the bump to prove it."

"There's just one thing to do," said Henny Penny.

"What's that?" asked Chicken Little.

"Sue the bastards!" said Henny Penny.

Chicken Little was puzzled. "Sue for what?"

"Personal injury, discrimination, intentional infliction of emotional distress, negligent infliction of emotional distress, tortious interference, the tort of outrage—you name it, we'll sue for it."

"Good gracious!" said Chicken Little. "What will we get for all of that?"

"We can get payment for pain and suffering, compensatory damages, punitive damages, disability and disfigurement, long-term care, mental anguish, impaired earning power, loss of esteem. . . ."

"Person, oh, person!" said Chicken Little joyfully. "Who are we going to sue?"

"Well, I don't think the sky *per se* is recognized as a suable entity by the state," said Henny Penny.

"I guess we should go find a lawyer and learn who *is* suable," said Chicken Little, her diminutive brain working overtime.

"That's a good idea. And while we're there, I can ask whom to sue for these ridiculously bony legs of mine. They've caused me nothing but anguish and embarrassment my whole life, and I should be compensated somehow for all that."

So they ran farther down the road until they came to the house of their neighbor, Goosey Loosey. Goosey Loosey was busy teaching her canine animal companion to eat grass so she could avoid the guilty feelings that came with feeding the dog processed animal carcasses from a can.

"The sky is falling! The sky is falling!"

"Sue the bastards! Sue the bastards!"

Goosey Loosey leaned over her fence and said, "Land sakes! Why are you two carrying on so?"

"I was playing in the road and a piece of sky fell on my head," explained Chicken Little.

"So we're going to find a lawyer to tell us whom we can sue both for her injuries and for my bony legs."

"Oh good! Can I come and sue someone for my long, gangly neck? You know, nothing really flatters it, so I am convinced there's a conspiracy within the fashion industry against long-necked waterfowl."

So the three of them ran down the road looking for legal assistance.

"The sky is falling! The sky is falling!"

"Sue the bastards! Sue the bastards!"

"Smash the conspiracy! Smash the conspiracy!"

Farther down the road they met Foxy Loxy, who was dressed in a blue suit and carried a briefcase. He held up a paw to halt the entourage.

"And what are you three doing out on this lovely day?" asked Foxy Loxy.

"We're looking for someone to sue!" they shouted in unison.

"What are your grievances? Personal injury? Discrimination? Intentional infliction of emotional distress? Negligent infliction of emotional distress? Tortious interference? The tort of outrage?"

"Oh, yes, yes," the three said excitedly, "all that and more!"

"Well, then, you're in luck," said Foxy Loxy. "My caseload has just eased up, so I will be able to represent you in any and all lawsuits we can manage to bring."

The trio cheered and flapped their wings. Chicken Little asked, "But who are we going to sue?"

Without missing a beat, Foxy Loxy said, "Who *aren't* we going to sue? Three hapless victims such as yourselves will be able to find more guilty parties than you can shake a writ at. Now, let's all step into my office so we can discuss this further."

Foxy Loxy walked over to a small black metal door that was in the side of a small hill nearby. "Step right this way," he said as he lifted the latch. But the black door wouldn't open. Foxy Loxy tugged on it with one paw, then with both. It still wouldn't budge. He yanked and pulled violently, cursing the door, its mental abilities, and its sexual history.

Finally the door swung open, and a huge ball of fire shot out. This was really the door to Foxy Loxy's oven! But unfortunately for him, the ball of fire engulfed his head, burned off every hair and whisker, and left him totally catatonic. Chicken Little, Henny Penny, and Goosey Loosey ran away, thankful that they had not been devoured.

However, the family of Foxy Loxy caught up with them. In addition to suing the manufacturer of the oven door on behalf of Foxy Loxy, the family brought suit against the three above-named barnyard fowl, claiming entrapment, reckless endangerment, and fraud. The family sought payment for pain and suffering, compensatory damages, punitive damages, disability and disfigurement, long-term care, mental anguish, impaired earning power, loss of esteem, and the loss of a good dinner. The three birds later brought a countersuit, and they've all been battling in court from that day to this.

THE FROG PRINCE

nce there was a young princess who, when she grew tired of beating her head against the male power structure at her castle, would relax by walking into the woods and sitting beside a small pond. There she would amuse herself by tossing her favorite golden ball up and down and pondering the role of the eco-feminist warrior in her era.

One day, while she was envisioning the utopia that her queendom could become if womyn were in the positions of power, she dropped the ball, which rolled into the pond. The pond was so deep and murky she couldn't see where it had gone. She didn't cry, of course, but she made a mental note to be more careful next time.

Suddenly she heard a voice say, "I can get your ball for you, princess."

She looked around, and saw the head of a frog popping above the surface of the pond. "No, no," she said, "I would never enslave a member of another species to work for my selfish desires."

The frog said, "Well, what if we make a deal on a contingency basis? I'll get your ball for you if you do me a favor in return."

The princess gladly agreed to this most equitable arrangement. The frog dived under the water and soon emerged with the golden ball in his mouth. He spit the ball on the shore and said, "Now that I've done you a favor, I'd like to explore your views on physical attraction between the species."

The princess couldn't imagine what the frog was talking about. The frog continued, "You see, I am not really a frog at all. I'm really a man, but an evil sorcerer has cast a spell on me. While my frog form is no better or worse—only different—than my human form, I would so much like to be among people again. And the only thing that can break this spell is a kiss from a princess."

The princess thought for a moment about whether sexual harassment could take place between species, but her heart went out to the frog for his predicament. She bent down and kissed the frog on the forehead. Instantly the frog grew and changed. And there, standing in the water where the frog had been, was a man in a golf shirt and loud plaid pants—middle-aged, vertically challenged, and losing a little bit of hair on top.

The princess was taken aback. "I'm sorry if this sounds a little classist," she stammered, "but . . . what I mean to say is . . . don't sorcerers usually cast their spells on *princes*?"

"Ordinarily, yes," he said, "but this time the target was just an innocent businessman. You see, I'm a real estate developer, and the sorcerer thought I was cheating him in a property-line dispute. So he invited me out for a round of golf, and just as I was about to tee off, he transformed me. But my time as a frog wasn't wasted, you know. I've gotten to know every square inch of these woods, and I think it would be ideal for an office park/condo/resort complex. The location's great and the numbers crunch perfectly! The bank wouldn't lend any money to a frog, but now that I'm in human form again, they'll be eating out of my hand. Oh, will that be sweet! And let me tell you, this is going to be a big project! Just drain the pond, cut down about 80 percent of the trees, get easements for. . . ."

The frog developer was cut short when the princess shoved her golden ball back into his mouth. She then pushed him back underwater and held him there until he stopped thrashing. As she walked back to the castle, she marveled at the number of good deeds that a person could do in just one morning. And while someone might have noticed that the frog was gone, no one ever missed the real estate developer.

JACK AND THE BEANSTALK

nce upon a time, on a little farm, there lived a boy named Jack. He lived on the farm with his mother, and they were very excluded from the normal circles of economic activity. This cruel reality kept them in straits of direness, until one day Jack's mother told him to take the family cow into town and sell it for as much as he could.

Never mind the thousands of gallons of milk they had stolen from her! Never mind the hours of pleasure their bovine animal companion had provided! And forget about the manure they had appropriated for their garden! She was now just another piece of property to them. Jack, who didn't realize that non-human animals have as many rights as human animals—perhaps even more—did as his mother asked.

On his way to town, Jack met an old magic vegetarian, who warned Jack of the dangers of eating beef and dairy products.

"Oh, I'm not going to eat this cow," said Jack. "I'm going to take her into town and sell her."

"But by doing that, you'll just perpetuate the cultural mythos of beef, ignoring the negative impact of the cattle industry on our ecology and the health and social problems that arise from meat consumption. But you look too simple to be able to make these connections, my boy. I'll tell you what I'll do: I'll offer a trade of your cow for these three magic beans, which have as much protein as that entire cow but none of the fat or sodium."

Jack made the trade gladly and took the beans home to his mother. When he told her about the deal he had made, she grew very upset. She used to think her son was merely a conceptual rather than a linear thinker, but now she was sure that he was downright differently abled. She grabbed the three magic beans and threw them out the window in disgust. Later that day, she attended her first support-group meeting with Mothers of Storybook Children.

The next morning, Jack stuck his head out the window to see if the sun had risen in the east again (he was beginning to see a pattern in this). But outside the window, the beans had grown into a huge stalk that reached through the clouds. Because he no longer had a cow to milk in the morning, Jack climbed the beanstalk into the sky.

At the top, above the clouds, he found a huge castle. It was not only big, but it was built to larger-than-average scale, as if it were the home of someone who just happened to be a giant. Jack entered the castle and heard beautiful music wafting through the air. He followed this sound until he found its source: a golden harp that played music without being touched. Next to this self-actualized harp was a hen sitting on a pile of golden eggs.

Now, the prospect of easy wealth and mindless entertainment appealed to Jack's bourgeois sensibilities, so he picked up both the harp and the hen and started to run for the front door. Then he heard thundering footsteps and a booming voice that said:

"FEE, FIE, FOE, FUM,
"I smell the blood of an English person!
"I'd like to learn about his culture and views on life!
"And share my own perspectives in an open and
   generous way!"

Unfortunately, Jack was too crazed with greed to accept the giant's offer of a cultural interchange. "It's only a trick," thought Jack. "Besides, what's a giant doing with such fine, delicate things? He must have stolen them from somewhere else, so I have every right to take them." His frantic justifications—remarkable for someone with his overtaxed mental resources—revealed a terrible callousness to the giant's personal rights. Jack apparently was a complete sizeist, who thought that all giants were clumsy, knowledge-impaired, and exploitable.

When the giant saw Jack with the magic harp and the hen, he asked, "Why are you taking what belongs to me?"

Jack knew he couldn't outrun the giant, so he had to think fast. He blurted out, "I'm not taking them, my friend. I am merely placing them in my stewardship so that they can be properly managed and brought to their fullest potential. Pardon my bluntness, but you giants are too simple in the head and don't know how to manage your resources properly. I'm just looking out for your interests. You'll thank me for this later."

Jack held his breath to see if the bluff would save his skin. The giant sighed heavily and said, "Yes, you are right. We giants do use our resources foolishly. Why, we can't even discover a new beanstalk before we get so excited and pick away at it so much that we pull the poor thing right out of the ground!"

Jack's heart sank. He turned and looked out the front door of the castle. Sure enough, the giant had destroyed his beanstalk. Jack grew frightened and cried, "Now I'm trapped here in the clouds with you forever!"

The giant said, "Don't worry, my little friend. We are strict vegetarians up here, and there are always plenty of beans to eat. And besides, you won't be alone. Thirteen other men of your size have already climbed up beanstalks to visit us and stayed."

So Jack resigned himself to his fate as a member of the giant's cloud commune. He didn't miss his mother or their farm much, because up in the sky there was less work to do and more than enough to eat. And he gradually learned not to judge people based on their size ever again, except for those shorter than he.

THE PIED PIPER
OF HAMELIN

he picturesque little town of Hamelin had everything a community could wish for—non-polluting industries, effective mass transit, and a well-balanced ethno-religious diversity. In fact, the town leaders had managed to legislate or intimidate away every element that could keep the citizens from living a good and sensitive life. Every element, that is, except the trailer park.

The trailer park on the edge of Hamelin was a civic embarrassment. Not only was it a terrible eyesore, with its rusted pickup trucks and trash heaps in every backyard. Within it dwelled some of the most unregenerate and irredeemable people you could ever imagine—murderers of nondomestic animals, former clients of the correctional system, and off-road bikers. With their plastic daisy pinwheels, loud music, and drunken weekend brawls, they sent a shudder through every respectable person in town.

One day, after a particularly riotous road rally through the trailer park, the town leaders had a meeting. After heated debate, they decided that somehow they had to eradicate the trailer park. But they were at a loss as to how to do it without ignoring or infringing upon the rights of the people who lived there. Finally, after even more oratory, they decided to let that be someone else's worry, since they were already so burdened with more important concerns, such as declining property values. So the town leaders decided to advertise for someone to solve their problems.

Soon after the advertisement was sent out, a man appeared in town. He was very vertically gifted and of lower-than-average weight for his size. His clothes were worn in combinations never before seen or imagined, and his mannerisms and high-pitched voice were certainly unique. Although he looked like he came from some world other than (but certainly not unequal to) our own, he gained the trust of the desperate town leaders.

"I will be able to rid your town of the trailer-park dwellers," said the man of enhanced strangeness, "but you must promise to pay me 100 pieces of gold."

The town leaders wanted this whole unpleasant business finished as soon as possible, so they readily assented. The sooner the trailer park was eliminated, the sooner they could all revert to their open-minded, progressive selves.

So the man of enhanced strangeness got down to work. He reached into his tattered knapsack and pulled out a sophisticated, compact recording machine. The people around him looked on with interest as he inserted a few tapes, set some knobs, and checked the sound levels. Then he began mumbling into the built-in microphone. No one could hear exactly what he was saying, but the man seemed to be lacking in coherence. Abruptly, he stopped mumbling, stood up, and told the town leaders that he needed a truck with a public-address system.

The authorities scrambled after this strange request. They managed to find such a truck at the

Department of Public Biodiversity and handed over the keys to the man of enhanced strangeness. He climbed in and drove off, popping the cassette he had made into the sound system. Everyone followed the truck as it headed toward the trailer park.

Soon music began to emerge from the slowly moving truck—generally country music but also occasional classics like "The Ballad of the Green Berets" and "Ghost Riders in the Sky." The town leaders were puzzled by this, until they noticed people emerging from their trailers, tool sheds, and taverns. The people had a certain glassy expression and talked to themselves as they stumbled along.

"I'm gonna go git me a job," said one. "I hear the carny is hirin'."

"I think I'll join the professional tractor-pull circuit," said another.

"Do you think I could make a livin' by signin' up for medical experiments?" asked a third.

The denizens of the trailer park followed the truck as it drove slowly toward the edge of town. Soon both they and it disappeared over the horizon, and the town leaders lifted a cheer.

About an hour later the truck returned, minus its entourage. "I led them all to the highway," said the man of enhanced strangeness as he alighted from the truck. "They're out thumbing rides for anyplace but Hamelin. Now the trailer park is free for you to use in whatever way you want."

"Marvelous!" said one of the authorities, who was serving as a spokesperson. "Now that they're gone, we can commence with our plans for a Third-World Refugee Reorientation Center. Thank you, thank you."

"Now, if you will kindly pay me the 100 pieces of gold you promised, I'll be on my way."

"Well, er . . . Hamelin is striving to establish an economy that is based on human capital and not the mere exploitation of physical resources. And so, to this end, we'd like to offer you this coupon book, which entitles you to such services in Hamelin as free massages and seminars on releasing your inner child."

The man of enhanced strangeness squinted his eyes. "You promised me 100 pieces of gold," he said, growing visibly angry. "Now pay up or suffer the consequences."

"If you wish to abandon your responsibility for making the world a more equitable place," clucked the spokesperson, "so be it. We will have to give you the official Hamelin IOU, which can be redeemed for a significant portion of its face value at many of the currency exchanges and liquor stores in the surrounding towns."

The man of enhanced strangeness paused, then chuckled eerily and climbed back in the truck. Before anyone could stop him, he began to drive through all the neighborhoods of Hamelin. As he went, the truck played a weird, high-pitched music that no one could recognize. Soon, the children of Hamelin emerged from their houses and streamed from their playgrounds. With glazed looks, they milled about in the streets. The town leaders could hear the children talking earnestly to each other:

"Free markets are the only sure way to give people the personal incentive to build a better society," said one child.

"We must respect the rights of citizens to preserve the ethnic purity of their neighborhoods," said another.

"Our only obligation as a society is to make sure everyone has a level playing field," said a third.

As their children began to form tax protest groups and gun clubs, the town leaders sadly realized that all their years of careful social planning would soon come to nothing. The next day, they found the public-address truck on the outskirts of town, but there was no sign of the mysterious man whom they had tried to swindle.

ONCE UPON A MORE
ENLIGHTENED TIME

Dedicated to Anne Conrad-Antoville,
principal cellist with the Eureka (California)
Symphony Orchestra, who chose compassion
over culture by resigning her position rather than
perform "Peter and the Wolf," an orchestral
work that teaches our pre-adults to fear and
despise wolves and other wild predators.

Also, and more importantly,
to Lies and Nyuji.

INTRODUCTION

At the outset, I would like to apologize sincerely for the success of my last book. The number of trees that voicelessly gave their lives so that my resource-greedy publisher and I could meet retail demand was truly appalling, and quite likely contributed to the global warming that gave those of us in the Northern Hemisphere such an unseasonably warm winter. We have made every effort to make this second volume more Earth-friendly, using natural soy inks, people-powered bicycle delivery systems, and photo-degradable paper that will revert to its basic organic components within a short time if exposed to light or read in the tub.

Next, I would like to apologize for exposing myself in my last book to be such an etymo-patriarchalist. As an alert reader in The Netherlands pointed out, while I used the proper spelling of the word "wommon" throughout *Politically Correct Bedtime Stories*, I still swaggered around, waving my phallocentric spellings of "person" and "human" in everyone's face. Properly penitent, in this volume I have opted to use the inclusive, gender-neutral spelling "persun." Unfortunately, a cultural-linguistic Catch-22 prevents me from using "hummon" or "hummun" because both spellings are rather nasty epithets in certain dialects spoken throughout the islands of Micronesia. Therefore, rather than offend those oft-oppressed and exploited peoples if and when this book is ever distributed in their region, I regretfully must choose to offend instead the oppressors and exploiters of the English-speaking world (you know who you are).

You hold in your hands another flawed yet earnest attempt to purge the "children's" stories popular in "Western" "culture" from the biases and prejudices that ran unchecked in their original "versions." Stretching as far back as Aesop and the Greco-Roman patriarchy he represents, I have chosen from a wide range of narratives based on familiarity and copyright protection. Sadly, space restrictions have forced us once again to omit "The Duckling that Was Judged on Its Persunal Merits and Not on Its Physical Appearance." I heartily apologize to all proponents of young waterfowl literature; please do not write or E-mail.

Once again, if through omission or commission I have inadvertently displayed any racist, sexist, cultural-ist, speciesist, socio-economicist, or other type of bias (including ism-ist divisiveness), I deeply apologize and stand open to correction. I am not and never claimed to be an expert, merely a citizen concerned with the effect of literature on our younger persuns. That I choose to use a book as the means to combat these influences may be ironic (irony itself being one of many suspect attitudes imported from the literary world), but it is the best effort I can muster at this stage of my persunal evolution. If this bibliocentric decision in any way offends, I ask you to find it in your heart, my enlightened reader, to forgive me.

A POLITICALLY CORRECT ALPHABET*

A   is an **A**ctivist itching to fight.

B   is a **B**east with its animal rights.

C   was a **C**ripple (now differently abled).

D   is a **D**runk who is "liquor-enabled."

E   is an **E**cologist who saves spotted owls.

F   was a **F**orester, now staffing McDonald's.

G   is a **G**lutton who says he's "food-centered."

H   is a **H**ermaphrodite skirting problems of gender.

I   is an "**I**sm" (you'd better believe it).

J   is a **J**ingoist—love it or leave it!

K   is a **K**ettle the pot can't call black.

L   is a **L**ifestyle not bound to the pack.

M is a **M**indset with bias galore.

N was a **N**egro, but not anymore.

O is an **O**ppressor, devoid of self-love.

P is the **P**atriarchy (see "O" above).

Q is a **Q**uip that costs someone a job.

R is the **R**easoning done by a mob.

S is a **S**exist, that slobbering menace.

T is a **T**eapot that's brewing a tempest.

U is for **U**mbrage at the slightest transgression.

V is a **V**alentine, tool of oppression.

W is for "**W**oman," however it's spelled.

X is a chromosome we share in our cells.

Y is a **Y**ogi for the easily led.

Z is a **Z**ombie, the differently dead.

* The traditional order of the letters in an alphabet is, of course, completely arbitrary. In spite of its association with excellence in archaic, competitive, literacy-obsessed school grading programs, A is no better or more deserving a letter than X, Y, or Z.

   Therefore, to deflect any criticisms of a noun-centric bias, I employed a random-letter generator before working on this new alphabet. Believe me, I was as surprised as anyone that, despite the tremendous odds, the random-letter generator spat out the alphabet in the exact order shown above.

HANSEL AND GRETEL

eep in a forested bioregion stood a small, humble chalet, and in that chalet lived a small, humble family. The father was a tree butcher by trade, and he was doing his best to raise his two pre-adults named Hansel and Gretel.

The family tried to maintain a healthy and conscientious lifestyle, but the demands of the capitalist system, especially its irresponsible energy policies, worked ceaselessly to smother them. Soon they were at a complete economic disadvantage and found themselves unable to live in the style to which they had become accustomed, paltry though it may have been. With the little money that was coming in, there was not enough to feed them all.

So, regretfully, the tree butcher was forced to devise a plan to be rid of his children. He decided to take them deep into the woods as he went about his daily work and then abandon them there. It was a sad commentary on the plight of single-parent households, but he could see no alternative.

When the father discussed this plan on the phone with his analyst, Hansel overheard the conversation. Instead of alerting the proper authorities, Hansel came up with a plan for protecting himself and his sibling. The next morning, the tree butcher packed them all sensible, nutritious lunches in reusable containers and they set off. Hansel, however, had filled his pockets with granola, and as they walked deeper and deeper into the woods, he dropped large chunks of it on the path to mark the way.

At a clearing deep in the woods, the tree butcher finally stopped and said to Hansel and Gretel, "You pre-adults wait here. I'm going to look for some trees to harvest, and maybe explore my primitive masculine psyche against the backdrop of nature, if I have time. I'll be back before too long." He handed the children their lunches and walked off.

After morning had turned into afternoon and afternoon into evening, Hansel told his sister their father's plan to abandon them. Gretel, always level-headed and practical in such situations, suggested they collect materials for a lean-to shelter, as they'd learned in their Outward Bound Aboriginal Survival Techniques class.

"No need," said Hansel. "I've left us a trail to follow back, without even littering or defacing a single tree." But when they went to find the trail, they discovered a cadre of survivalists busily eating up the granola. The survivalists screamed at the children to get away from their newfound rations and, after firing a few warning shots in the air, disappeared into the woods.

Hansel and Gretel wandered along different trails, but after some time they became hopelessly lost and very hungry. Then, around a sharp bend in their path, they came upon a wondrous cottage made of carob brownies, sugarless gingerbread, and carrot cake. Even without a reassuring FDA label, the cottage looked so good that the children dived at it and began to devour it.

Suddenly, a wommon in her golden years (actually, quite past them) emerged from the cottage. The many bangles on her wrists and ankles clattered as she moved, and she gave off the aroma of patchouli, burnt sage, and clove cigarettes. The children were startled. Hansel asked, "Please forgive my bluntness, but are you a wicked witch?"

The wommon laughed. "No, no, my dear. I'm not a witch, I'm a Wiccan. I'm no more evil than anyone else, and I certainly don't eat little pre-adults, like all the rumors would have you believe. I worship nature and the Goddess, and mix herbs and natural potions to help people. Really. Now why don't you both come in for a nice cup of coltsfoot tea?"

Inside the functional yet edible cottage, the Wiccan advised the children to forget the propaganda and slander that had been spread about persuns like her. She told them stories about her life in the forest, making potions, casting spells, communing with non-human animals, and healing the many wounds inflicted on Mother Earth. It took some time for Hansel and Gretel to free their minds from the stereotype of a green-skinned, temporally advanced crone in a pointy black hat. (Ironically, the Wiccan did have a long warty nose that resembled a moldy cucumber, but the children were too polite to ask about it.)

They were finally convinced of the Wiccan's sincerity when they met her neighbors and kinsfolk. To welcome the children, these gentle people held a gathering that night in the moonlight, in which they stripped off all their clothes, rubbed mud on each other, and danced in a circle to the sound of ocarinas and panpipes. It was an inspiring sight, and it felt so right and natural that Hansel and Gretel decided then and there to give up their old lives and join the forest people.

Over time, Hansel and Gretel came to love the Wiccan and their lives in the forest. As they grew older and more empowered, they began to assert their bonds with Mother Earth in more direct and tangible ways. With courage and vigor, they planned and engaged in many deep ecology actions to protect their arboreal home. Hansel and Gretel merrily spiked trees, monkey-wrenched mining and bulldozing equipment, and blew up power plants and electrical lines that stretched over nearby farmland with explosives made from all-natural ingredients. They even learned 15 completely organic remedies for powder burns.

They were very content and self-fulfilled protecting their adopted habitat until one day terrible news came. A huge multinational paper conglomerate had purchased their entire forest, intent on turning it all into wood pulp. Hansel, Gretel, the Wiccan, and all their compadres and com-madres geared up for the confrontation of their lives. The eco-defenders gathered up their wrenches and their plastique, their picket signs and their panpipes, and started off for the headquarters of the conglomerate, alerting the media along the way that they were ready to defend Our Mother to the very last persun.

Hansel, Gretel, and the Wiccan marched at the head of the crowd, chanting and swaying and itching for a fight. As the headquarters of the paper company came into view, the two siblings saw something about it that was very familiar. The huge plant and building complex took up nearly four acres of land, but on the circular driveway, smack in the middle of the main entrance, sat a small, humble chalet. It was in fact their childhood home, squatting like a hermit's shack in front of the sleek steel and glass facade of the HQ.

Just as the brother and sister were beginning to digest this, the small wooden door of the shack opened and out stepped their father, the tree butcher. He was dressed in an Armani suit with Italian loafers, and on either side of him crowded a phalanx of lawyers. It was obvious that the woodspersun had done OK for himself.

"Well, well," said the father, "the wheel of fate spins round again. Good to see you again, Hansel and Gretel."

"Please, don't call us that," said his biological but not spiritual son. "We have changed our names to symbolize the birth of our new consciousness and to separate ourselves from our heartless, exploitative upbringing. From now on, you may call me Heathdweller."

"And my name is Gaia," said his sister.

"Change your names to Thumper and Bambi, for all I care," their father laughed. "You people are still going to have to relocate from the forest. We've made a deal with a nice trailer park down by the Interstate for you, and hired a relocation counseling firm to help—"

The Wiccan cut him off. "Death to the rapers of Earth! Death to the rapers of Earth!" she screamed, and the rest of the crowd picked up her chant.

"No need to get personal," the father muttered. He moved to calm the crowd. "All right, all right. We'd like to meet with your spokesman—"

"Spokeswommon!" insisted one protester.

"Spokespersun!" shouted another.

A lawyer whispered into the father's ear. "We'd like to meet with your persun of spoke," the father said finally, "the Wiccan."

Amid shouts of encouragement the Wiccan raised her fist and walked into the building with the suits. The ecoteurs were very happy and confident because they placed their complete trust in the Wiccan. She would never back down in the face of these planet ravishers. To celebrate, they formed a prayer circle in the parking lot and began to dance.

The sound of ocarinas and panpipes was still in the air when the negotiators reemerged from the building. The father and the lawyers were smiling, while the Wiccan had a more sheepish expression, although it is an insult to sheep to imply that they could ever look so guilty.

Gaia, née Gretel, immediately sensed that something in the established order of things had changed. "What's happened?" she insisted. "What went on in there?"

"A prominent member of your group has decided to wake up and face reality," said her father. "The Wiccan has agreed to join our senior staff, as our new Vice President of Holistic and Spiritual Wellness, Mother Earth Division."

An involuntary gasp escaped from the eco-warriors. "How could you?" screamed Gaia.

"Child, I had no choice," she said in a pleading manner. "They gave me complete medical and dental, including experimental cures that most policies won't cover."

A confused murmur went up from the eco-squadron. This was indeed a stunning blow. If their wisest and most earth-conscious persun-in-arms could be so easily bought, what chance did the rest of them have? Along with the lawyers around him, the tree butcher wore a grin like the cat that had satisfied its nutritional needs at the expense of the canary.

But Hansel—oops!—Heathdweller and Gaia were well acquainted with their father's ruthlessness and had devised a back-up plan. With great pomp and flurry, they each put on hooded robes, drew a penta-gram on the ground, and burned dried herbs in a small crucible. Everyone looked on in curiosity, and perhaps with a little fear. Then the brother and sister chanted an invocation in a language that even the Wiccan had never heard. The wind began to blow and the air crackled. Then, with a flash of light, it was done. The entire papermaking operation—headquarters building, plant, and warehouse complexes—had changed from steel and concrete to peppermint sticks, gingerbread, and gumdrops.

The ecoteurs' mouths hung open, then they let out a cheer. The lawyers conferred among themselves and jotted notes about possible action plans in their Filofaxes. The Wiccan just stood there while her mouth formed a silent "Wow."

The tree butcher put on a brave front. "Nice trick, kids, but you haven't stopped me. The plant is still as sturdy as ever, and now my maintenance costs are down to a little frosting and fudge. Thanks very much. We'll still keep operating, and we're still going to tear down your forest."

Heathdweller and Gaia didn't answer him, but instead burned more herbs and breathed more incantations. The wind again blew and the air crackled, and before everyone's eyes, the entire squad of lawyers was turned into a horde of mice—very *hungry* mice—who immediately swarmed over the huge, sticky-sweet industrial complex that lay before them and began to devour it.

The Wiccan had no idea that the siblings were so well versed in the black arts. She tried to appease them with flattery: "That was very impressive. We have a lot to teach each other, don't we? I'm looking forward to sharing our knowledge together in an open and supportive—" but her words were cut short as Heathdweller and Gaia flicked their paranormal whip and transformed her from a wommon in her golden years to a slinky, white-bellied weasel. The former Wiccan then ran off to join the mice in their factory feeding frenzy.

Their father was now visibly shaken as he watched the work of a lifetime being squeakily devoured. Ever the master of the guilt trip, he finally said, "And this is how you kids repay me? Do you think it was easy being a single working parent? If I hadn't brought you into the woods that day, you wouldn't have found this whole new life for yourselves. And this is the thanks I get? What about my needs? I've been in the wood business all my life, now what am I supposed to do?"

So Heathdweller and Gaia did him a favor and turned him into a beaver.

After this ordeal, the ecoheroes picked up their placards and headed back into the forest.

Heathdweller and Gaia worked hard at perfecting their supernatural skills, which they put to use solely for defending the planet. Their neighbors respected the siblings' privacy, lest a stray incantation turn them into a different (though certainly not inferior) species. And the magickal brother and sister, their friends, and, most important, the trees of the forest lived happily ever after.

THE ANT AND THE
GRASSHOPPER

n the world of the ancient Greeks, agriculture was still in a state of advanced rudimentariness. The farm ecosystems were diverse and healthy, with indigenous free-range plants and thriving insect colonies sharing space with the domesticated crops. As a result, the fields of wheat and grapes were filled with a variety of vigorous, forward-looking, and well-spoken insects. The most industrious of these was the ant. All summer long he worked in the hot sun, storing away grain and seeds in anticipation of a long winter.

In that same field lived a grasshopper whose life was very free from care, since he had long ago rejected the bourgeois, money-grubbing concept of "making it." To him, the ideal existence was to enjoy Nature in an unstructured and playfully exploratory manner, and he often took advantage of His/Her/Its beneficence by sleeping most of the day. At other times, he would sing joyfully in the meadow, *churREEP churREEP*, thus keeping alive the rich oral tradition of the grasshoppers.

This alternative attitude did not go unnoticed by the ant, as he toiled in the heat and dust. When he saw the grasshopper enjoying life on his own terms, it made every orifice in his exoskeleton cinch up tight.

"Look at that grasshopper," the ant muttered to himself. "Sitting around on his abdomen all day, singing his blasted songs. When will he ever show some responsibility? To call him a leech would be an insult to all the hardworking segmented worms in this country. He's just watching me, waiting for the chance to jump me and take everything I've worked so hard for. That's the way it is with his phylum."

For his part, the grasshopper was also watching the ant, but with an entirely different train of thought.

"Look at that ant," he mused, "working so hard to accumulate his little store of grain. And for what? If only he would try to be a little more Zen-like. He might understand that, to the stone, one kernel of grain is the same as one thousand, and the rain never has to worry about its penmanship."

So the summer went. The ant, a quintessential type-A persunality, worked himself into a frenzy every day, but his selfish and socially irresponsible activity took its toll. He developed a peptic ulcer, had some scares with thorax pains, and lost most of the hair on the top of his head. In mid-September, his wife left him and took the pupae, but he scarcely noticed. The ant became so obsessed with his store of grain that he went so far as to install an elaborate security system in and around his anthill, with video cameras and motion sensors to catch any would-be thief.

In between naps, the grasshopper watched all this with detached curiosity. He also studied hatha yoga, scoured the area for the perfect cup of cappuccino, taught himself to play the guitar (really only one song, a self-penned, quasi-blues number with three notes), and generally hung out. He tried to keep his leisure-centric lifestyle attuned to the passing of the seasons. When the weather turned less congenial, he planned to go to Australia and do a little surfing.

But winter arrived early that year (or summer left too soon, depending on your climatic orientation) and the fields were quickly barren. The unfortunate grasshopper found himself a victim of the capriciousness of meteorological change. He went hopping about the field, looking for sustenance of any kind. He would have settled for a crumb, a husk, a bit of tofu—but nothing edible could be found.

Soon the grasshopper spotted the ant, lustily dragging a full cornstalk behind him. The grasshopper's hunger got the better of his pride, and he walked over, intending to ask the ant to share a little of his immense hoard. But as soon as he caught sight of the grasshopper, the ant began to scream.

"AAAHHHHH!!! What do you want? What are you doing here? You've come to take my cornstalk, haven't you? I know you've been plotting the day when you would snatch away everything I own! Your type are all the same!"

The grasshopper tried to interrupt, but the ant raved on: "Don't say anything! Don't try to work your wiles on me, with your sob stories and empty promises! I've worked hard for what I have, even if that might not be fashionable in some circles."

The grasshopper said politely, "But surely, Brother Ant, you have more than you could ever possibly eat."

"That's my business," said the ant, "and we don't live in some blood-sucking socialist state . . . *yet!* Get with the program, grasshopper! The only place where success comes before work is in the dictionary."

"I was planning to go to Australia, see, but the weather, like, *changed* and all the food has disappeared. . . . "

"That's how a free market works, pal. Take a lesson."

"Forgive me, Brother Ant, but I feel obliged to say, like, I think you need to work on your karma. The aura you're giving off is full of negative energy, which you could easily convert into positive by simply—"

"Look, you want to get all mystical on me, then tell me: What's the sound of one bug starving? Ha ha!"

The ant and the grasshopper were interrupted in their fruitless debate by the sound of a cough. They turned and saw a huge mantis bigger than the two of them put together! (The mantis was at one time a praying mantis but had been prohibited from such practices by court order. He did, however, retain a deeply spiritual side.) The ant and the grasshopper were frightened, not by the mantis's larger-than-proportionally-average size but by the nonsense-free aspect of his appearance. He wore a gray polyester suit and brown loafers with tassels, and in his forelegs he carried a briefcase, a brown paper lunch bag, and a calculator.

"Ant?" the mantis asked, even though he knew exactly which one he was looking for. "Ant, I've come for an audit."

With those six ominous words, the course of our story changes. Omitting the details of the audit, and the contested charges, and the suit and countersuit, and the ant's attempted flight to the Caymans, suffice it to say that the greedy insect's hoard was appropriated and put to more responsible community uses after he was enrolled in the correctional system. The grasshopper, meanwhile, organized a program for young area insects eager for cultural interchange with countries with warmer climates. Thanks to government revenue redistribution (and the ant's estate), the grasshopper has been directing surfing expeditions from that day to this.

THE PRINCESS AND
THE PEA

n a kingdom over the hills and far away, there lived a young prince who was very full of himself. He was healthy, relatively handsome, and had had more than his fair share of happiness and comfort growing up. Yet he felt that he deserved something more. It was not enough for him to have been born into a life of parasitical leisure and to keep the masses firmly under the heel of his calfskin boot. He was also determined to perpetuate this undemocratic tyranny by marrying only a real, authentic, card-carrying princess.

His mother the queen encouraged her son's obsession, despite the obvious risks of hemophiliac or microcephalic grandchildren. Many years earlier, after a period of inadequate wellness, his father the king had achieved corporal terminality. This lack of a strong male presence gnawed at the prince on a subconscious level, and no amount of weekend retreats and male bonding with other young dukes and barons could relieve this anxiety. His mother, for her own codependent and Oedipal reasons, did not bother to change or correct his selfish notions of unattainable perfection in a spousal lifemate.

In his quest for the perfect partner, the prince travelled far and wide, looking for someone to enslave in matrimony. Astride his trusty equine colleague, he went from kingdom to queendom and from dukedom to duchessdom, asking for names and phone numbers. Heavily or lightly pigmented, vertically or horizontally challenged, cosmetically attractive or differently visaged—he cared not a whit. His only criterion was the royal authenticity of a wommon who could share his regal delusions of privilege and persunal worth.

One rainy night, after a long journey to many

far-off bioregions, the prince nourished himself with a bowl of lentil-curry stew and confided his fears to his mother: "I don't think I'll ever find a genuine princess with whom to share my life, Mummy."

"Well, Son," the queen reassured him, "don't forget the many benefits of the single life. Don't let society and the church pressure you into a life-style for which you might not be suited."

"Perhaps I should widen my scope a bit," he mused.

"What? And throw out your standards?"

"No, Mummy, perhaps I have fallen into a trap of the orthodox heterosexualist majority. Maybe there is a fine young *prince* out there for me. It's at least worth a try."

Before his mother could answer, there was a knock on the castle door. The servants pulled open the heavy portal, and out of the rain stepped a young wommon, who was moisture-enhanced from head to foot. She was certainly attractive to the eye, if you're the type of shallow persun who attaches value to appearances. Luckily for our story, the prince was not one of those types. He had one standard, and only one standard, classist though it may have been.

Imagine the prince's surprise when the visitor blurted out, "A princess shouldn't be out in weather like this!" Well now, *this* was a revelation straight from the equine animal companion's mouth! The prince was struck orally inoperative for a moment, then invited the dryness-challenged visitor to enjoy their hospitality in the castle overnight.

While this was certainly a joyous development for the prince, his mother felt very threatened that someone was taking her son away from her. But rather than acknowledging the validity of her feelings and airing them in a constructive way, the queen decided on a ruse to test the visitor's claim.

She sneaked up to the bedchambers and found the room where the persun of saturation would be sleeping. She tore off all the bedding from the frame and placed one single pea on the bed slats. Then she placed 10 futons on top of the pea, and on top of that, 10 eiderdown quilts.

"There," said the queen. "If that drenched wench downstairs is really a princess, she will be refined enough to notice this lump and be unable to sleep."

The next morning at breakfast, over the royal granola, the queen innocently asked the young wommon how she had slept.

"Abominably," she replied. "I didn't get a wink all night."

The queen's eyes grew wide. Had her plan worked too well?

The visitor continued. "First of all, the bed was piled high with eiderdown quilts. Barbaric! How could I sleep, thinking of the poor geese who unwillingly surrendered their feathers for my comfort?"

The queen reddened a bit but said nothing.

"Then, as I was removing all the extra futons to share them with some of the less fortunate peasants living around the castle, I found a pea placed beneath them all. Shocking, with the state of the world as it is, that someone would waste food like that."

With these statements, the queen nearly choked on her soy milk. The prince, who had learned of his mother's scheme to screen out a princess, was so excited he couldn't keep silent any longer. "So you really are a princess!" he yelped.

"Last night I was, yes," she replied. The quizzical looks from the prince and queen led the wommon to elaborate: "Last night I was a princess; this morning I am an ancient Viking warrior. Oh, you sillies—I'm channeling! I have over a dozen past personalities that periodically inhabit my body—everyone from Charlemagne's mistress to Aesop's brother-in-law. And Cleopatra. But then, everyone's been Cleopatra at some time or other. Let me tell you, it makes for some interesting conversation at parties! It's all pretty exciting for an economically disadvantaged spoonmaker's daughter who grew up on the wrong side of the drainage ditch."

These revelations made the queen very angry, but the prince was intrigued. "So, when do you think you will be channeling a princess again?"

"A week from Tuesday," she said matter-of-factly, "mid-morning until early evening. I am very punctual with my past lives."

"Then on that Tuesday afternoon, I will ask you to be my wife and castle-mate, and you can rule by my side as an equal partner in every way."

The wommon considered a moment, then answered: "I would accept, if not for the fact that this morning, as I have said, I am a Viking warrior—Liefdahl by name, son of Ülfdahl—and I have a strong notion to lay siege to your castle just after breakfast." She calmly took a sip of coffee and grabbed another muffin.

"How rude!" said the queen with a slap on the

table. "We give her lodging in a storm and breakfast the next morning, and she swaps personalities on us and calmly talks about laying siege to us, without so much as a 'by your leave'!"

"Mother, please," said the prince. "Now, how long are you generally a Viking warrior?"

"Oh, not longer than 45 minutes."

"And after that?" he asked.

"After that, I'm usually St. Giles, living in a hovel and renouncing all worldly possessions."

"And that would include . . . ?"

"That would include"—the visitor smiled with a dawning awareness—"renouncing any and all worldly kingdoms conquered by my other spiritual co-habitators."

So, as is often the case, timing was crucial to a happy ending to our story. The "princess" and the prince were married the second Tuesday following, in accordance with her metaphysical timetable, and they had a very happy honeymoon, especially during certain transformations. Every time she became Liefdahl, son of Ülfdahl, she would conquer the prince and his castle, and every time she became St. Giles, she would give it right back. Channeling past lives and historical personalities became *de rigueur* in court from that day forward, and the queen, the prince, and the channeler lived a very happy life together, never quite knowing who would turn up at breakfast.

THE LITTLE
MER-PERSUN

 way from the land, far from the shore and the effluent from stinking cities and corporate farms, was a habitat unlike any other in the world. Below the ocean surface, the plants grew in clusters of pink and red and yellow, and the long grasses swayed slowly in the current. Among these swam a host of colorful fishes, crustaceans, and arthropods in a stunning example of a healthy food chain. And amid all this teeming life flourished another race of creature, a unique and magnificent incarnation of biodiversity: the mer-people.

The mer-people had a king, and this king had seven daughters who all embodied to some degree the standards of attractiveness prevalent at that time. The one who best embodied these, however, was the youngest, who was named Calpurnia but nicknamed Kelpie. She was a very happy young sea-citizen, and she had the most pleasant singing voice that the mer-people had ever heard. She and her sisters were very close, and they all spent many hours collecting recyclables and jamming the sonar of whaling vessels.

The seven princesses loved to hear stories from their grand-mer-mother, especially about the mysterious folk who lived above the water's edge. Their grand-mer-mother told them about the old merchant ships that flew by, the forests and meadows filled with strange creatures, the bustling cities populated with persuns. The princesses could scarcely imagine such a place. They all laughed when their grand-mer-mother told them how the land people moved around on teetering pink stilts (those who were temporarily abled, of course) with fancy coverings on the ends to protect the stilts from wear. Their grand-mer-mother admonished them not to laugh at those unlucky enough to be born finless, but the princesses flicked their long tails and wondered how the land creatures could stand to look at themselves in the mirror.

The more stories they heard, the more curious the mer-sisters became. However, they were forbidden by mer-custom to swim to the surface on their own until their 15th birthdays. They weren't happy with this arrangement, but for the sake of cultural harmony, they agreed to abide by this restrictive rite of passage.

As the youngest in the family, Kelpie watched each of her mer-sisters swim to the surface on her 15th birthday and return with wondrous stories. One told of how humans were obsessed with making machines that saved themselves labor, then spent lots of money in special clubs for the privilege of keeping their muscles toned. One told of how they cut huge holes in their biggest trees, so they could examine Nature closely without leaving the comfort of their smoke-spewing metal sleds. One told of how the people built expensive electronic machines to help themselves sing in strange, shadowy places called karaoke bars.

But the little mer-persun was only mildly interested in learning how the other half breathed. She was content to explore her damp yet secure world, play with the fish and other sea citizens, and grow in the confidence of her own mer-persunhood.

Soon the date of her 15th birthday arrived, and Kelpie was finally going to get her chance to view the surface world and engage in an open-minded cultural exchange. Since this rite of passage was as important from a sociological standpoint as her puberty in general, her mer-sisters and grand-mer-mother fussed over her greatly. Kelpie was generally not very vain, but she let her mer-kin adorn her with red seaweed, glittering coral, and bright oyster shells (always, of course, with the consent of the oysters). After all, there were so few rituals that feminine mer-persuns could call their own.

Bedecked in her finery, the little mer-persun swam away from her palace home toward the surface. The sun grew brighter and yellower as she rose, but the water also became murky and full of debris. When she finally broke through the surface, for the very first time in her life, she felt as though she needed a bath.

My, is it noisy above the water! she thought to herself. There were engines roaring, horns blowing, people shouting, and water splashing in a terrible cacophony. As she searched for the source of the din, she spun around and saw behind her a huge ship whose crew was firing powerful water hoses at a group of bearded men in a small rubber raft. The big ship was festooned with huge nets, cranes, and rigs, and the bearded men seemed to be steering their raft directly into its path. Kelpie was alarmed by the spectacle, but she had no idea what a life-and-non-life struggle it was until one man in the raft stood up and was knocked into the sea by a mighty blast from a water hose.

Always an altruistic sort, Kelpie dived without thinking and swam to rescue the man, who thrashed and screamed in the water. She came up from below and caught him just as he began to sink. When they made it back to the surface, he looked at his savior and could scarcely believe his eyes.

"Am I dead, or am I just crazy?" he asked.

"You're not dead, obviously," she said, "but as far as your mental health, I would leave such a diagnosis to a qualified professional."

"But you're . . . you're a mermaid!"

"Listen, buster," she said, the scales rising on her back, "another sexist remark like that and I'll let you swim home."

"No! I'm sorry, I wasn't thinking!"

"'Mer-persun' is the common term," Kelpie advised him, "although in my opinion it emphasizes the human part of our makeup at the expense of our fishness. It's an ongoing debate, you understand."

The little mer-persun examined this strange creature carefully. His hair was thicker in some places than in others, but unlike that of the otter or the sea elephant, it was scarcely enough to keep him warm or buoyant, and he was sorely blubber-deficient besides. His discomfort was obvious from the deep shade of purple his lips were turning.

"I must get you back to land before you freeze," Kelpie said. "Why were you pushed off your boat, anyway?"

"We were protesting drift-net fishing, and that Russian trawler decided that they could do whatever they wanted to us, since we were in international waters. But we got the bastards on videotape, so they're in trouble now."

She thought to herself, *What a strange phrase, "international waters,"* then said to him, "Your efforts to defend the ocean's ecosystem are commendable, but you almost became shark food yourself."

He looked dreamily into her eyes. "None of that

matters now. You are the most beautiful creature I have ever seen."

"Oh, don't talk bilge."

"What's your name? Mine's Dylan."

"My name is Calpurnia, but my friends call me Kelpie."

"I am so taken by your beauty and kindness, Kelpie. I love you. I want to stay with you forever."

"It wouldn't work. See, your fingers are already turning pruney."

"But if I can't stay here, why don't you come live with me? I can make my house mer-accessible with flumes and chutes. I could even introduce you to Phillipe Cousteau—he can make you a star."

"Hold on, finless," she said, turning angry. "You air breathers are really full of yourselves, aren't you? You don't love me. You just want to show me off to all your friends. 'See what an eco-friendly stud I am? I'm living with a mer-persun!' Why in all the sea would I want to join your private aquarium? I can hear the jokes now: 'Where can I get me some of that bait?'; 'I love a little tail'; 'Hey, baby, wanna spawn?' Forget it, Greenpeace boy, I'm not some trophy you can claim from the sea and mount."

The surface dweller didn't have much of anything

to say after this. His teeth were chattering and his eyes were glazing over as he reached the more advanced stages of hypothermia. Even with his terra-centric attitude, the mer-persun felt pity for Dylan in his primate-out-of-land position, and she headed for shore as fast as she could. Meanwhile, the men on the rubber raft successfully stopped the Russian trawler by jamming the raft into its propellers and causing a boiler to explode aboard ship, which sent all the crew members and the ecowarriors to a watery yet commendable grave.

The little mer-persun, dodging sinister drift nets and massive, churning cruise ships, tried to find a secluded shoreline where she could throw the human back. However, rampant beachfront and wetlands development made this nearly impossible until she found one rocky cove with a small sandy beach. Before the man could wake up, Kelpie swam off, not wishing to endure any more emotional scenes, cultural imperialism, or Jungian archetypes.

Back home she told her whole mer-family about her adventures on the surface. Of course, she left out Dylan's profession of love and his ideas for a life together, which (the more she thought about it) involved nothing but great sacrifice on her part and numerous benefits for him. Besides, Kelpie found the whole idea rather repulsive. Her mer-family applauded her selfless, she-roic efforts.

Some months passed and the little mer-persun gave barely a thought to the air breather she'd saved. She was too busy with her music lessons and her algae garden to consider a relationship with someone who wore clothes and walked on two feet.

One day a courier from the castle swam up to Kelpie in her garden and breathlessly announced that her presence was desired in court immediately. Wondering whatever could be the matter, she hurried to the royal hall. There she found her mer-father, her grand-mer-mother, her mer-sisters, and many royal advisers and drifters-on. And in front of the mer-king swam a strange pink creature—bulky and armored and shaped like a macaroon.

"Daughter, come forward," intoned the mer-king in a properly regal tone. "This visitor requests an audience with you." When the stranger drifted around, Kelpie's jaw nearly hit bottom. It was Dylan, the eco-defender she had saved from drowning!

"Greetings, Kelpie," he said.

"Dylan! But what . . . what's happened to the rest of you?" she asked.

"I've had myself turned into a denizen of the sea. It's amazing what they can do with gene splicing these days."

"But in the name of Poseidon, *why?*"

"To prove my sincere devotion and love for you, of course."

"No, I mean, why did you choose to become half-man, half-*prawn*?"

Dylan sighed. "It's a long story, involving government restrictions on research and chromosome compatibility and so forth. But I gotta tell you, I love my new hard shell and eyestalks. Look, I can read both pages of a book at the same time!" He demonstrated his new ocular talents for everyone assembled.

"But you've sacrificed your peopleness," Kelpie said. "What about your family and friends?"

"Who needs 'em? Buncha primates. I've always felt more at home on the ocean, only now I'm *in* the ocean. And today, seeing you here in the salt water, I love you even more."

"I'm very touched. I . . . I don't know what to say," she stammered, utterly captivated by his deep and selfless sacrifice.

Dylan turned to face the throne and summoned

up all the dignity he could in his bulky pink frame. "Your Majesty, I'd like to ask for your daughter's hand in marriage."

The mer-king replied royally, "What kind of sexist operation do you think we're running here? Ask her yourself, shrimp."

He turned to the little mer-persun and asked, "Calpurnia, will you marry me?"

What could Kelpie say but yes? She could've said no, she wanted to continue her education and establish a career. She could've said no, she didn't approve of scientific augmentation or changes between species. She could've said no, she was allergic to shellfish. She could've said no a thousand different ways, but happily she said yes.

Kelpie and Dylan were married soon after that and begat a fine school of fry. In a few years time, Kelpie became more involved in affairs of state and sang occasionally for the entertainment of their friends, while Dylan continued his eco-defense activities, this time from below the water. And while their life together wasn't a bed of coral every day, they always taught their spawn to be happy and proud of their multi-cultural, multi-genus heritage.

THE TORTOISE AND THE HARE

f all the boastful and self-important animals, the worst in all the countryside (apart from the humans, of course) was the hare. He would talk on and on about his swiftness, sleekness, and superior muscle tone with anyone unfortunate enough to be nearby. What's more, he continually derided the other animals that didn't share his obsession with fleeting physical "perfection."

One of his frequent targets for ridicule was the tortoise, who with his stout yet functional legs, lower metabolism, and overall endomorphic body shape stood (or rather squatted) in marked contrast to the hare. The tortoise, perfectly content to take on life at his own speed, always insisted his metabolism was as efficient as anyone else's.

The hare, however, continually taunted the tortoise while he struck poses and flexed his pecs. "Hey, low-rider," he said, "I bet you can make extra money (*huff-huff*) renting yourself out as a paperweight (*huff-huff, preen-preen*)!"

The tortoise smiled patiently. "Thank you for the advice, my velocity-fortified friend."

"Come on, stumpy," goaded the hare, "can't you rise up when someone (*huff-huff*) throws down the gauntlet?"

"I can't see how gauntlet abuse has anything to do with me," said the tortoise, who had apparently achieved slowness in more than one aspect of his character. "I enjoy my inertia and would rather just sit and watch the world go by."

"Ooooh, how can you be so content?" fumed the hare. "You're just so smug (*huff-huff*), I challenge you to a race to show you the consequences and (*preen-preen*) health risks of such a sedentary lifestyle."

The tortoise was appalled. "A . . . *competition?*"

He almost choked on the word. "Just to prove that one of us is somehow *better* than the other? What kind of example is that to set? I'll have no part of it."

Some other animals that were standing nearby overheard this conversation and began to listen with interest.

"What's the matter (*preen-preen*), are you . . . ?" The hare caught himself and looked around, then said in a softer voice, "Are you chicken?"

At this, the tortoise grew angry. "Now listen, if you're going to start insulting other species to cover up your own insecurities . . ."

"Come on, doorstop," taunted the hare. "Are you really compassionate for pullets or just plain scared?"

A crowd of animals had now gathered and was, to use another poultry-exploitative phrase, egging on both combatants. Some were eager for the hare to be put in his place, others wanted to see the tortoise's self-righteous bubble popped, and still others were the unreflective couch-potato types who craved constant stimulation.

With pressure coming from all sides, the tortoise felt a tug-of-war between his principles against competition and the need to teach the hare a lesson. Finally, and without a trace of irony, he said, "All right, I'll race you. And what's more, I'll win, just to prove to you that winning isn't everything."

Preparations for the big event began immediately. The tortoise and the hare agreed to appoint the fox as Commissioner of Kinetic Wellness and Overland Velocity Contests. It was the fox's duty to establish the route and duration of the race, as well as work out the details for the merchandising and pay-per-view revenue. There was some talk about adding biking and swimming meets to the footrace, but it was decided that interest in such an "Iron Animal" competition wouldn't be as high.

The hare and the tortoise began to train in earnest for Race Day. Some ignorant commentators assumed that all members of the rabbit family were fast, due to their genetic inheritance, limber body, and well-developed thigh muscles. The hare rightly took exception to these prejudices because they ignored his many hours of hard work and sacrifice. To counter them, his training camp was always open to the media and his supporters, who cheered him on as he cross-trained. This also kept the persistent rumors of blood-doping and amphetamine abuse to a manageable and deniable size. For his part, the tortoise prepared by carbo-loading and watching training films.

As the hype for the big showdown escalated, the imagination of the other animals in the countryside was absolutely (and somewhat unhealthily) focused on the race. Depending on their individual temperaments, the animals were rabidly and obsessively either pro-tortoise or pro-hare. Many a friendship, marriage, and other significant interanimal relationship was tested in the days leading up to the race.

The hare zealots—generally more youthful animals who were impressed solely by style, speed, and hipness—strutted around in specially licensed T-shirts with the slogans "Just Jump It" and "Rabbitude!"

Fans of the tortoise praised his defense of principle against tremendous odds, as well as his self-deprecating wit and acceptance of his alternative body image. They expressed their support by donning baseball caps stitched with the words "Eat my dust, bunny!"

A small but vocal non-majority opposed the entire notion of holding a race at all. They wrote op-ed pieces, phoned in to radio talk shows, and even distributed a poster that read, "RACES are not HEALTHY for kids, colts, kittens, pups, chicks, ducklings, cygnets, eaglets, hatchlings, calves, cubs, fawns, lambkins, piglets, joeys, tadpoles, and other living things." Their efforts were to no avail, however, and the day of the big race soon arrived.

The air crackled with anticipation that morning as the crowds gathered at the starting gate. Vendors were there, selling chipatis, juices, and energy-supplement bars. Promoters were there, giving away phone cards, sports drinks, and cereal samples emblazoned with pictures of the tortoise and the hare. Newscasters and TV technicians were there, in droves of elaborate electronic vans, to exploit every last detail and image of "this story about the simplest of all challenges—to race."

Hardly anyone noticed when the tortoise arrived. He was so unassuming and free of ostentation that he blended in easily with the crowd. The serene look on his face was puzzling, considering the long odds he was up against.

As you might expect, the arrival of the hare and his entourage could not be described as humble or restrained. It was hard to miss the long black limousine that edged its way through the crowd, or the cheers that erupted when the doors flew open and out stepped the hare, with a starlet on each arm and surrounded by four beefy bodyguards (or animal protection professionals, as they preferred to be called). The rowdier elements of the crowd tried to get close to the hare, but his muscular interdiction force kept them at bay.

The hare stepped up to the starting line, raised his hands to the crowd, and took off his gold lamé warm-up suit. He gulped a big swallow of the sports drink he was endorsing and ate a fistful of his authorized breakfast cereal with a smile. He then turned to the tortoise with a menacing look in his eye.

"I'm gonna pound you so bad, tortoise, (*huff*) it'll make lying on your back feel like a vacation."

Whether or not he meant to offend any of the optically challenged members of the crowd, the tortoise just smiled and said, "We'll see."

The starter for the race, having been enjoined not to use a pistol, a cannon, the word "BANG!" or any other violent inducement to run, held a red handkerchief at arm's length, let it hang there a few seconds, then dropped it with a flourish. Instantly, the hare was off in a lightning blaze of speed. The tortoise moseyed off at a more natural pace, ever mindful that most sports injuries arise from inadequate preparation and abrupt starts and stops.

With cheering throngs on either side, the hare sped down the course like quicksilver. By the time he was out of town and in the countryside, he had long lost sight of his competitor. So confident was he in his velocity prerogative over the tortoise that he decided to accept the invitation of one of the film crews and grant an interview about his mid-race thoughts, reminiscences of childhood, and hopes for the future.

Meanwhile, the tortoise plodded on, carefully replenishing his bodily fluids with the cups of isotonic liquid that were provided along the route. He soon found himself hitting what runners call "the wall," but the encouragement from the crowd and his own strength of will helped him push through it until he entered the "zone." It was a good thing, too, since at that point he was only 30 meters from the starting line.

The hare chatted amiably about himself with the interviewer and, since he was talking about his favorite subject, the time flew by. When it was all wrapped up and the hare stepped out from the trailer, he heard cheering coming from the direction of the finish line. He bounded down the course, touched by the idea that the crowd was warming up to welcome him. But when he finally caught sight of the end, what did he see but the tortoise crossing the finish line!

The hare ran as fast as he could, but he couldn't pass the tortoise in time and had to settle for "finishing almost fastest." He began to scream and pound his fists, complain about the officiating, demand a recall of the commissioner, challenge the tortoise to a urine test, and threaten to sue for millions in lost endorsement revenue. The tortoise just wanly smiled as he tried to power down.

Meanwhile, to celebrate the victory, fans of both the tortoise and the hare, as well as various bystanders and hangers-on, smashed shop windows, looted electronics and jewelry stores, overturned cars, and set fire to anything that was handy. By the time the police broke up the crowds with recycled rubber bullets and biodegradable pepper gas, they had arrested 57 animals for over-enthusiastic celebrating.

While such destructive merrymaking was deplorable (and certainly depended on many socioeconomic influences), the most shocking part of the story was yet to come. Both racers did submit to urinalysis, and the results were not good for the tortoise, who was found to be a heavy user and abuser of steroids. The tortoise claimed that it was really the aftereffect of an asthma medication, but the fox, in his role as Commissioner of Kinetic Wellness and Overland Velocity Contests, was forced to disqualify him and proclaim the hare as "finishing most fastest."

In response to this scandalous news, fans of both the tortoise and the hare, as well as various bystanders and hangers-on, smashed shop windows, looted electronics and jewelry stores, overturned cars, and set fire to anything that was handy. This time the police arrested 115 animals for over-enthusiastic celebrating.

It was soon decided that footraces, pawraces, hoofraces, and other such competitions only inflamed the animal populace and unleashed emotions that were not nurturant of public harmony. The fox resigned his position and was immediately named the new Facilitator of Constructive, Cooperative Kinetic Pastimes. His department heavily promoted participation in noncompetitive activities such as snorkeling, water ballet, hackey sack, and duck-duck-goose (for any and all species). Further, he decreed any animal found to be competing with his or her neighbor in any type of sport or contest was to be disciplined with several hours of community service and forced to listen to audiotapes of the various sportscasters giving their analysis of the big race between the tortoise and the hare.

PUSS IN BOOTS

n a land not so very far away lived a man and his three sons. After the father had achieved his inevitable non-essentialness, his estate was divided among his sons: The eldest inherited the oil company, the next eldest got the publishing and media holdings, and the least eldest got a cat. Forgetting for a moment the hours of companionship and contentment that an animal companion can bring, the least eldest son pleaded with his brothers not to compel him to contest the will in probate.

"Listen, brothers," he said, "while you'll be able to support yourselves with your share of the inheritance, I'll be lucky if I can breed this cat or put it in commercials. Don't force me to sell him to a cosmetics company just to get a return on my assets."

His brothers ignored him and told him to have his lawyer call their lawyers, but the cat obviously took offense at these flip remarks. Later the cat scolded this cruel, shortsighted human: "It's just like your kind to treat someone with four legs like a resource for you to exploit. We're not put here for your enrichment, bub, material or otherwise. In fact, I'm so disgusted that now I'm not going to tell you how I was going to make you a great and powerful persun."

More than the fact that the cat could speak, these last words sparked the interest of the ambitious yet meagerly synapsed young man: "Oh, Mr. Puss, my dearest and most trusted friend, how did you plan to do this?"

"I don't think you want to know. You obviously haven't the foresight and fortitude it would take for a successful career in public service."

"Oh, please," said the winningly eager young man. "I'd love to go into politics. I'm not much suited for anything else, and my brothers might be able to give us a jump-start in the contributions area."

The cat sighed. "My heart does go out to you," said Puss, "a poor idiot left on his own. Very well, I will help you. For me to get started, I need two things: first, a blue pinstripe suit—Armani, nothing less—plus a briefcase and some fancy stitched cowboy boots; and second, a promise that you'll never make a single solitary utterance in public without my OK."

The wholesome-looking young man readily agreed, since he never had much that was important or original to say anyway. He took the cat to a fancy haberdasher to be outfitted properly. When this was done, the cat told him, "Go home now and wait. Practice looking statesman-like by riding horses, playing touch football, writing your memoirs, things like that."

"But I don't have any memoirs to write," protested the ruggedly handsome young man.

"I said *practice* writing," the cat reiterated, pointing a claw. "If you think you'll ever have the chance to do your own writing, then we've got a problem already." With that, Puss in Boots left to call his first press conference.

The primaries for the senate race were only five weeks away at this point, and the field of candidates was already quite crowded. When Puss in Boots held his press conference, only a handful of reporters had the time or interest to show up. This hardly mattered, since it was to be rather short anyway.

All the cat did was walk to the podium and say, "I'd like to announce that my employer is not a candidate for the party nomination for the senate seat at this time. Thank you. No questions, please." Then he walked away.

And was the reaction tremendous! Breathless articles and news reports began to appear about the reluctant candidate. Who was he? What did he stand for? What was the significance of the public groundswell that surrounded this strapping figure of youthful vitality? With just the slightest spin doctoring and some wise use of media time, Puss in Boots proceeded to forge the image of his human companion as a man forced into public life by the will of the people, who were disillusioned and were looking for a white knight (colorist though such concepts are) on a tall fiery charger (ditto heightist and speciesist, not to mention quite Eurocentric overall).

Within a few weeks and without uttering a word, the young man with the Redfordesque good looks won the party nomination for the senate!

"Wow! I can't believe it," said the malleable candidate. "I guess I'd better start figuring out my position on the issues."

"You do and I'll break your neck," hissed the cat. "Let me worry about your positions, as well as your beliefs and your off-the-cuff remarks and your spontaneity and everything else. You just remember: Don't say a thing unless I tell you to."

Now Puss in Boots began to work in earnest to get his meal ticket elected to the senate. He issued position papers that were totally pointless yet exquisitely quotable. He had the candidate photographed shaking hands with factory workers, retirees, and customers at luncheonettes. They challenged the incumbent to a debate and then backed out at the last minute, declaring that such an event would be just an exercise in "politics as usual." Their optimistically simple campaign slogan—"It's Time for a Change!"—seemed to strike a chord with the optimistically simple voters.

Throughout the frenzy of the campaign, no one noticed or commented on Puss in Boots's lack of credentials. In fact, seduced by his easy and apparently candid manner, no one ever noticed that he was of feline descent at all. It just demonstrated the commentator's observation, "In the land of the optically challenged, the monocularly gifted individual is first in line at the trough."

Election day drew near, with all the mudslinging and innuendo you could imagine. Puss in Boots's candidate, however, with his easy confidence and glint in the eye, seemed somehow to rise above the fray. This might have been due to the fact that he was still forbidden to speak his mind (or what there was of it) in any way, shape, or form. Puss in Boots, on the other hand, was always available to the media and ready with a charming, folksy anecdote or some evidence that their opponent had undergone electroshock therapy to stop the temporary lapses into dementia that made him want to release all the criminals from prison with a $50 gift certificate and an automatic pistol.

As the campaign came down to the wire, and with his heartland–born-and-bred candidate lagging in the polls, Puss knew it was time to stop playing footsie. He called another press conference and this time announced to the media, "Our campaign honorably requests that our opponent step down from the race, so that we won't have to disclose possible evidence we may have found that might link our opponent to

an experimental, gender-reversing medical proce-
dure he may have undergone 23 years ago in an
undisclosed overseas country, where the majority of
the population speaks Swedish. Thank you. No
questions, please."

This insinuation, as you may have guessed, turned
the entire campaign around. Rumors flew about the
type of evidence Puss and his boss may or may not
have had. Their opponent repeatedly denied accusa-
tions that he had once been a wommon and was
now a man, that he was still a wommon now trapped
in a man's body, or that he was now a man trapped
in a wommon's body with a penchant for cross-
dressing—not that there is anything wrong or unnatural, certainly, with any of these lifestyle choices.

As usual, emotions rather than reason carried the
day, and after all the ballots were counted on election
day, Puss in Boots and his ruddy, exuberant human
companion had won by a comfortable margin.

At the victory party, Puss pulled the new senator
aside and said to him, "You see? I told you I could be
useful to you. You may not have the wealth of your
brothers yet, but you soon will have, and even more
clout, if you play your cards right. There is even
some talk—initiated by me, of course—that you're

going to run for president in the next election because the country's problems are too urgent and your ideas are too big to be penned up in the senate. What do you think of that?"

"Oh, my skillful, cunning cat," he said, "I can't thank you enough. Please accept my apologies for ever contemplating selling you to perfume researchers."

"Just do as I say," said Puss in Boots, taking a sip of his designer water, "and instead of the stealth candidate, they'll be calling you . . . Mr. President. Now, you better get up there and give them the victory speech I wrote for you."

The beaming politician entered the crowd to cheers and applause and pushed his way forward to the podium. "To my family, friends, and supporters," he began, "I want to thank you all for your hard work and dedication, and I'm pleased to tell you I have just received a phone call from my opponent conceding the election!"

Applause, applause, applause!

"He was a worthy adversary and fought the good fight, but this campaign was not about issues or ideology, or even ability or brainpower. It was about the plain and simple message: It's time for a change!"

Applause, applause, applause!

"And now, if you'll let me, I'd like to depart from my prepared comments." From the wings came the sounds of a glass shattering and a low, painful groan. He continued, "I'd like to thank someone without whom this victory wouldn't have been possible: my campaign adviser, my confidante, and I'm proud to say, my cat—Puss in Boots!"

Applause, applau . . . *silence.*

Had they heard him right? This Kennedyesque young man, their bright and shining knight, their hope for the future, had let his *cat* run the campaign? Not that it was unprecedented—other non-human animals had held high appointed positions for years—but why had he kept it a secret? What kind of a man was he to hide such information, and what else was he hiding?

"Puss," he said, "come out here and take a bow."

Puss in Boots just stood in the wings, shaking his head, his paw over his eyes. He had had his doubts, but he never wanted to believe his master was so cerebrally undercapitalized as to spill the legumes at his own victory party.

The people in the crowd grew angry, even the cat lovers. They felt they'd been deceived, cheated, jilted, cuckolded. They started to boo, tear down banners, and pop balloons as they began to look for payback. The new senator had to make his escape through the rear behind the rostrum. He looked for his cat everywhere with no luck. Then, over in a corner, he saw a group of reporters and cameras gathered around, and there was Puss in Boots right in the center of them.

By the time the senator got to where the press had clustered around Puss, all he could hear was his cat saying, " . . . to apologize to everyone who worked on this campaign and put their trust in this candidate, and also to you, you hardworking reporters. Had I known this pathetic schemer to be so . . . unstable and . . . duplicitous, I would never have become involved with his campaign. I hereby resign from his staff before any other damage is inflicted on the electoral system, or on the hearts and minds of the public. Thank you. No questions, please."

The reporters ran off to file their stories. Puss in Boots walked slowly up to his former employer and said, "If only you'd stuck to the script. Good luck in office, if you survive the recount."

"But I don't understand," said the beleaguered senator. "No one figured out you were a *cat* before now?"

Puss looked him straight in the eye. "Do the words 'credibility problem' mean anything to you? Nobody really *cares* that I'm a cat—not on the record, anyway—but now because of your slip of the brain, it looks like a big cover-up. Fraud, nepotism, interspecies exploitation—your squeaky-clean image is kaput. If you *had* to tell them, a weepy confession would've been much better than a bungled disclosure. That's Spin Doctoring 101, but you're working with such low wattage, it slipped right by you."

Puss in Boots bid the man farewell and walked away. He wrote a few magazine articles to tell his side of the sordid story, then got a job as a television pundit based in the capital. The senator barely survived the inevitable recall vote, but questions about his judgment lingered and impeded any effectiveness in office he might have had over the next six years. Almost from the day he was sworn in, he was treated like a non-ambulatory waterfowl, something Puss in Boots reminded him and the rest of the country about every time the pundit cat went on the air.

SLEEPING PERSUN OF BETTER-THAN-AVERAGE ATTRACTIVENESS

ong, long ago, there lived a king and a queen, two equal partners in life who shared everything—including the fervent wish to have a baby. (This was much easier for the king, of course, since he would never have to endure the upheavals of pregnancy, the pain of childbirth, and the miseries of postpartum depression. You could rightly call his wish more vicarious than hers.) But as many times as the king would

inflict his baser instincts on the queen, they (or, more accurately, *she*) remained childless.

One day, as the queen bathed in a nearby river, a frog leaped onto the lily pad next to her. Then, to her amazement, the frog cleared its throat and spoke.

"Although it's probably not a good idea to bring another human being into the world," said the amphibious messenger, "I know of your conception problems and would like to help. If you follow my advice, you will soon be with child."

"Oh, such joyous news!" trilled the queen. "What must I do to prepare myself, frog?! What must I do?! Tell me!!"

"Your best bet is to go the natural route, and for pity's sake, learn to relax! Get some regular exercise, eat more greens and grains, and eliminate animal fat from your diet. Later, if you need one, I can recommend a good lactation consultant."

So the queen did as the frog directed, and on the next full cycle of the moon, her body was colonized by the seed of the exploitative monarchy.

Nine months later (not to minimize the physical strain on the queen in the interim), a healthy pink pre-wommon was welcomed into the castle. Many gender-neutral names were considered for her, such as Connor, Tucker, and Taylor, that might have lessened any sexual discrimination she would encounter on her career path (for, while she was born a princess, her parents would never presume to limit her future to one of mindless leisure and privilege). After talking to a few image consultants, they decided to give her the name Rosamond.

The king was so happy and so proud of his now-obvious potency that he ordered a huge banquet to be held. Special guests from all over the kingdom came and feasted on exotic fruits, rare vegetables, and whole-grain casseroles (although nobody touched the lovely placenta paella). The most special of all the guests were 12 magickally accomplished womyn, famous throughout the land for their wisdom and their rejection of the hegemony of analytic Western rationalism. After the feast, each wommon walked up to the persun of newbornness and gave her a blessing.

"May this pre-wommon be blessed with a body image with which she is comfortable," said the first.

"May she have a keen analytical mind that also leaves room for intuition and inspiration," said the next.

"May she have good math skills," said the third, and so on down the line.

But either through oversight or superstition, the king failed to invite the 13th member of this magick sorority. Humiliated by this snub, she snuck into the gathering and hid in the shadows, nurturing her resentment. When she could stand it no longer, she pushed her way to the center of the crowd and was up-front with her emotions: "So you think you can create the perfect persun with all your blessings? Not if I can help it!" She strode up to the royal bassinet and said to tiny Rosamond, "May you grow up thinking you can't be complete without a man, put unrealistic hopes of perfect and total happiness on your marriage, and become a bored, dissatisfied, and unfulfilled housewife!"

Everyone in the room gasped in fright! How could anyone be so morally out of the mainstream to wish such a terrible fate on a defenseless child? The 13th wommon cackled in a manner that just happened to be maniacal and, ignoring everyone's pleas to stay and talk through their differences, disappeared into the shadows.

Luckily for little Rosamond, the 13th magickal wommon had long ago rejected the validity of empirical scientific thought, and as a result had forgotten how to count. The vengeful sorceron did not realize that the *12th* magickal wommon had not yet given her blessing on the child. While this wise and kind sister could not undo what had been done, she could lessen the agony of this terrible curse. She walked up to the pre-adult and said, "When you are just reaching the prime of puberty, may you prick your finger on a spinning wheel and fall asleep for 100 years. By that time, perhaps men will be more evolved and your pain in finding a progressive, affirming lifemate will not be so great."

With all these supernatural blessings, curses, and overrides, the king became so fearful for his daughter that he ordered every spinning wheel in the kingdom destroyed. Deprived of a means of producing any fabric, the people of the kingdom were forced to devise new ways of reusing old clothing, and thus reduced their conspicuous consumption and eased the burden on their landfills.

As the years passed, Rosamond grew into an intelligent, compassionate, and self-actualized young wommon. Whether she was also physically attractive is of no importance here and also depends entirely on one's standard of beauty. It also perpetuates the myth that all princesses are beautiful, and that their beauty gives them liberty over the fates of others. So, please, don't even bring up the fact that she was quite a looker.

One day, when her parents were off on a retreat to learn to release their "inner peasant," Rosamond began to explore her castle. She came upon a doorway she had never seen before, which led to a winding stairway up into a tower. At the top of the tower was a little room, where Rosamond found a temporally advanced wommon busy at her spinning wheel.

"What are you doing, sister?" Rosamond asked.

"Recapturing the means of production and staking ground in my own economic empowerment," she replied sweetly.

"It looks like fun, yet also educational and enriching; may I try?" But no sooner had Rosamond touched the wheel than her finger was severely pricked. And before she could decide whether alyssum or lobelia tincture would make the best balm for the wound, she fell into a deep state of non-wakability.

And at the instant Rosamond fell asleep, in an inspiring display of solidarity, everyone in the castle also began to slumber. The environmental hygienist stopped scrubbing the floor, the domestic engineer stopped dusting, the laundron stopped washing the clothes, and all fell asleep right where they were. Even the nonhuman animal residents—while they certainly weren't bound to obey or emulate the humans—stopped in their tracks and nodded off.

Around the castle the grounds were left untouched and reverted to their natural wildness. As the castle's inhabitants slept, thorn bushes grew thickly and heavily year after year, so that soon they blocked passage to the castle and eventually obscured it from view entirely. This vibrant new bio-district would have gone unmolested, if not for the lustful and destructive natures of the males in the surrounding kingdoms. Legends grew about the castle and the sleeping princess therein—who now had become an unsurpassed beauty in the wish-fulfilling stories that the men recounted. Many young princes, in a rush of hubris and testosterone, sought to disrupt the thorny ecosystem and awaken the princess, as if she were just some windup doll waiting for the man with the right key. But no sooner did these foolhardy adventurers push their way through the vegetation than the thorn bushes closed tight, ensnaring the men until they returned to the earth from which they came.

Then, after 100 years, through the region rode another prince (and please don't ask how charming he was, either). He had heard about the environmentally friendly castle and its REM-enhanced inhabitants, and was intrigued by the idea of a place so at peace with itself. He dismounted from his trusty equine companion and walked up to the thick hedge. With a creak and a rustle, it opened to let him pass, and he walked through its verdant portal. Once inside the castle, the prince marvelled at the stillness around him. All the people, all the animals, all the birds—even the fire in the grate—were perfectly motionless. Amazed by all this self-control, the prince believed he had stumbled upon a top-notch meditation center and rejoiced, for he was a pilgrim dedicated to self-improvement and transcendence to the Absolute Reality. He began to search the grounds for the sensory deprivation tanks, then found the door to the tower and ascended the stairs.

When he opened the door to Rosamond's room and saw her lying there, the prince marvelled at her serenity and composure. He knew immediately that she was the one responsible for the enlightenment of the castle. Eager to learn from such a venerable mistress, he touched her on the arm, then tapped her, then poked her, then shook her, then jostled her. "She is in such a deep meditative state that the outside world completely falls away for her," said the prince. "Oh, I must follow this teacher!" To show his reverence, he crawled to the foot of her cot, kissed her slippered foot, and settled into a lotus position.

Immediately Rosamond began to stir. She coughed and smacked her lips numerous times, trying to get rid of the taste of 100 years of morning mouth. She sat up and saw the figure sitting at the end of her cot, and instantly something changed inside her. All of Rosamond's independence, education, and previous persunal growth fell away like a cloak, and she swooned like a starlet in a cheap melodrama. "My prince, you have awakened me!" she chirped loudly.

The prince was awestruck. He didn't realize what he had done, and hardly had the breath to say, "Oh, I beg your forgiveness, teacher. I did not want to disturb your meditation. I seek only your guidance . . ."

"But I am not your teacher," she giggled. "I am your princess, and you have come to take me away from all this, make me your bride, bring me to a big castle with a white picket fence, and let me live happily ever after!"

"Take you away? From this Shangri-la, this Utopia? But your entire castle is a huge vortex of positive energy, the perfect place to expand our consciousness and pursue individual nothingness."

"What are you talking about? Come and kiss me!"

"Kiss you?" he asked in a very disappointed voice. "Oh, teacher, how carnal! You do not think me worthy of enlightenment."

"But you are the only man who could arrive here and break the spell," she cried. "We were fated to be together."

"Teacher, you should know there is no such thing as fate," corrected the prince, "only our unique destinies, and if we are lucky, a little synchronicity thrown in here and there."

"Don't use such big words," Rosamond pouted. "Didn't you come here to marry me and make me a fulfilled wommon?"

The prince thought for a second, then looked panicked. "Teacher, please! Your riddles are too much for a neophyte such as I. Be patient with me, I beg you."

"A hundred years is long enough to be patient," she insisted. "It's bad enough that none of my friends will be alive to come to my wedding, but on top of that, I get a prince who doesn't want to get physical, only metaphysical."

The prince looked supremely lost. This was certainly not how he'd envisioned a meeting with an exalted teacher. "I don't know about you," he said with a sigh, "but I could really go for a nice, soothing colonic."

The frustrated Rosamond begged the prince to be her mate, but her tears, bribes, and threats could not move him. The prince, who wanted to get in touch with his own emotions rather than hers, continued to beseech her for her knowledge and insights (which were rather scanty, as you might understand, despite her 116 years on the planet). With their arguing, they stayed up long into the night, as did the rest of the castle after such a monumental catnap. And so, with this sad standoff, the prophecies of the 12th sister of sorcery, as well as those of the 13th, were fulfilled.

THE CITY MOUSE
AND THE SUBURBAN
MOUSE

 mouse who lived in the suburbs had an old friend who lived in the city. One day he invited his friend to come out for a visit. The city mouse readily accepted the invitation, eager to see his pal and enjoy some greenery for a change. So on the duly appointed day, he walked to the central mass-transit dispatch point and took a train out to the end of the line.

Upon arrival in the suburbs, the city mouse began to look for his friend's house. Of course, he was used to straight, numbered streets and quickly got lost amidst the wide lawns, curving roads, and cul-de-sacs. After several hours of searching through the Valley Dales and Dally Vales, the Nettle Brooks and Breton Nooks, by sheer luck he found his friend's address.

The suburban mouse had gone to great lengths to make this a memorable visit, even buying a big floral centerpiece to match the napkins and placemats on his table. He'd laid out a sizable feast for his guest— macaroni and cheese, creamed corn, even Jell-O salad with mandarin orange wedges. The city mouse ate a bit of each dish but couldn't help showing his disdain for such mundane fare. The unnatural quiet was also beginning to get to him; the only sounds he could hear were the clicks of lawn sprinklers and the roar of distant riding mowers. After dinner, the suburban mouse handed the city mouse a no-alcohol light beer and suggested that they do a little channel surfing to pass the time.

The city mouse said, "My friend, life is too short to live this way. Look at you! Your food is dull, your entertainment is dull, even your hairstyle is 15 years behind the times."

The suburban mouse was taken aback, especially by the comment about his hairstyle. "Heavens, what should I do?"

"Come visit me in the city next week," was the reply, "and we'll enjoy more diversity and excitement than you've ever dreamed of. I'll show you the life that's fit for a healthy young mouse!"

So the next week, the suburban mouse headed into the city. He was a little late arriving because it took him 2½ hours to find a parking space. As he stepped out of his car, he was asked for a monetary donation by someone supporting himself outside the reigning capitalist paradigm. The vehement language and uncompromising natural aroma of this street citizen startled the suburban mouse, who fell over backward into the gutter. After he picked himself up from the grime, two police officers began to harass him about interfering with the "quality of life" in the neighborhood and inquired whether he would be so kind as to refrain from showing his stupid face around there again or he'd be buying himself a mess of trouble. The suburban mouse sagely took their advice and trotted away. A half-block away from his friend's apartment, the visitor was interrupted by a former client of the correctional system, who liberated the mouse's watch and wallet in return for the gracious offer of letting him walk away in one piece.

Shaken, sore, and spun around, the suburban mouse finally reached his friend's building. No sooner had he done so than the city mouse ran down the front steps.

"Where ya been? C'mon, we'll be late for our dinner reservations."

"But I," he squeaked breathlessly, his paw over his heart, "I was just mugged and—"

"Ah, fuhgetabouddit!"

And the two of them rushed off to dinner. The city mouse had chosen a new, exclusive restaurant that combined the cuisines of Jamaica and Tibet in an original way (its most popular dish was the jerk yak). There was a long line of customers waiting outside the restaurant, but the mice enjoyed a private dining area in the alley by the kitchen. They feasted on scraps of some of the finest and costliest fare in the entire city. The suburban mouse didn't recognize any of the food, and wouldn't have been able to pronounce the names if he had, but he was thoroughly enjoying himself. His earlier troubles faded into the background as he gobbled away hungrily next to his friend. Then they slipped out for cappuccino and cannolis.

The suburban mouse was entranced by all the activity and diversity around him—all the yelling and laughing, cars honking, music playing. Nighttime in the city seemed even more vibrant and alive than daytime in the suburbs. A vast, wonderful panorama he never knew existed was unfolding before him with dazzling speed.

On the way home, in front of the tropical pet and retread tire store, a pair of unlicensed sex workers tried to engage them in conversation. "Hey, fellas, how about a little transaction in the personal services sector?" said one with refreshing candor about the true nature of all male-female relationships.

The suburban mouse thought this was all marvelously colorful and authentic, and he began to ask the sex-care providers where on earth they went shopping for their boots. The city mouse, not wishing to cause a scene, grabbed his friend's arm to lead him away and continued walking. Just past the 24-hour copy shop and marital aids emporium, a man came up to try and sell them some watches. The suburban mouse thought one of the watches looked suspiciously familiar, but still they kept walking. Finally, on the street where he had parked his resource-guzzling, air-befouling automobile, he could find no trace of it.

"They . . . they towed away . . . " he stammered.

"Ah, fuhgetabouddit!"

Five floors up, in the city mouse's studio apartment, they capped their night off with a bit of Armagnac. The city mouse said, "See the excitement you're missing, living way out in the sticks where you do?"

"Oh, I do, I do," the suburban mouse said earnestly. "This has all really opened my eyes. Life here has so many possiblities! I can never thank you enough for such a wonderful night!"

"Ah, fuhgetabouddit!"

"No, really, this has been a groundbreaking evening," said the suburban mouse. "I feel so alive! It feels like life is a huge Broadway musical and I've got the chance to play the lead. This evening has allowed me to accept things I never have before. And I'm so grateful to you that I want you to be the first to know. I'm . . . I'm coming out of the wainscoting."

"You're what?" asked the city mouse.

"I'm attracted to other mice," he said.

"Well, it's a good thing, seeing as you're a mouse and everything."

"No," said the suburban mouse, "I'm talking about mice of my own gender."

After an infinitesimal pause, the city mouse exclaimed, "That's great! Thank you for sharing that with me. It's not exactly my piece of cheese, you understand, but I applaud your acceptance of who you are. If I can help in any way—help in a *general* sense, that is—don't hesitate to ask."

"Since you mention it," the suburban mouse said, "would you allow me to stay here with you until I can sell my baseboard in the suburbs?"

Although the city mouse didn't really have enough room in his place, what could he do but welcome his friend and lend him support as he embarked on his new life? Tempers flared a few times, such as when the city mouse scratched a couple of his friend's Judy Garland records, but things went smoothly overall. In a few months, the ex-suburban mouse found his own place downtown, as well as many new friends and interests. And every

Halloween the city mouse and the ex-suburban mouse got together for the big parade and celebrated another life saved from the shackles of monotonous middle-class conformity.

POLITICALLY CORRECT
HOLIDAY STORIES

Dedicated to the good persuns of Moorhead State University, where mistletoe has been officially banned as a holiday decoration, because, according to school president Roland Dille, it "tends to sanctify uninvited endearment."

Also, to Lies and Liam,
my shining Christmas stars.

INTRODUCTION

Fluffy white snow. Cups of golden eggnog. Visions of sugar plums.

At this festive time of year, it is good for each and every one of us to consider carefully just how cruel and exclusionary so many of our old seasonal "traditions" continue to be. To place so much emphasis on snowfalls and a "White Christmas" surely is a slap in the face for those persuns in developing tropical nations, who never get to see snow firsthand. The friendly offer of a cup of eggnog is nothing less than a poke in the eye to the dedicated vegans among us. And anyone recovering from an eating disorder can certainly attest that visions of sugar plums dancing in one's head are more like a nightmare than a sweet dream.

Because of the callousness and insensitivity that abound during the holiday season, I felt compelled once again to perform a public service in the name of right-thinking celebrants everywhere and revise the favorite seasonal tales for our more sensitive era.

To avoid any suggestion that with this book I am cashing in on the holiday's consumer feeding frenzy, let me mention that I tried to persuade my publisher to bring this volume out at a more sedate time of year, such as February or March, when everyone could discuss these emerging ideas calmly and rationally. But the book was made ready for autumn publication because we agreed that one more old-fashioned holiday season is one too many.

To all those cynics who believe that a responsible and progressive celebration must also be differently enjoyable (i.e., no fun), I would ask them to consider the evolution of current traditions. We are all aware (or should be) that the early Christians chose to celebrate the birth of their savior at the same time as pagan winter festivals that welcomed the return of the sun. They were thus able to celebrate "Christ's mass" without alienating their neighbors and doubled their chances of being invited to a tasty feast at the same time. Such an early example of inclusionary merrymaking should inspire us all. Today's neopagans can feel especially proud of their heritage/himitage.

We can also turn the holidays into opportunities for positive critical thinking by taking instruction

from many legends and oral traditions. Consider the
senior lifemate's tale about the animals imprisoned
in the barnyard, who are granted the gift of speech
on Christmas Eve. Initially we might look on this as
a disturbing attempt to anthropomorphize other
species, forcing them against their will to celebrate
the holidays of human animals at the neglect of their
own traditions. However, we can turn this fable into
an exercise in positive self-reflection if we try to
imagine the insights the animals might reveal to us
about our own species. Whether we like what they
have to tell us, of course, is another matter.

It is certainly regrettable that this task of liberating
the holidays from the oppressiveness of tradition has
not been undertaken before, and that it has been left
up to a member of my race, class, and gender to
complete. To employ the symbols of the season, I do
not consider myself a wise man, a shining star, a
lamp of miraculous oil, a feast of first fruits, a heav-
enly messenger, a piñata, or any type of magickal log
or fiery pudding. I hope to avoid any impression that
I pattern myself after that other member of the
Genital Power Elite, Kris Kringle, barging in and
assuming that my "gifts" will be gratefully accepted
by right-thinking persuns everywhere. My only wish

is that you will enjoy these stories and share them with your family, alternative household, or other social or non-social group. I hope they will become a new tradition for you, at least until something better comes along. And may your holidays be whatever you decide to make them, if indeed you make them anything at all.

'TWAS THE NIGHT BEFORE SOLSTICE

T was the night before solstice and all
through the co-op
Not a creature was messing the calm
status quo up.

The children were nestled all snug in their beds,
Dreaming of lentils and warm whole-grain breads.

We'd welcomed the winter that day after school
By dancing and drumming and burning the Yule,

A more meaningful gesture to honor the planet
Than buying more trinkets for Mom or Aunt Janet,

Or choosing a tree just to murder and stump it
And dress it all up like a seasonal strumpet.

My lifemate and I, having turned down the
    heat,
Slipped under the covers for a well-deserved
    sleep,

When from out on the lawn there came such a
    roar
I fell from my futon and rolled to the floor.

I crawled to the window and pulled back the latch,
And muttered, "Aw, where is that Neighborhood
    Watch?"

I saw there below through the murk of the night
A sleigh and eight reindeer of nonstandard height.

At the reins of that sleigh sat a mean-hearted
    knave
Who treated each deer like his persunal slave.

I'd seen him before in some ads for car loans,
Plus fast food and soft drinks and cellular phones.

He must have cashed in from his mercantile chores,
Since self-satisfaction just oozed from his pores.

He called each by name, as if he were right
To treat them like humans, entrenching his might:

"Now Donder, now Blitzen," and other such aliases,
Showing his true Eurocentrical biases.

With a snap of his fingers, away they all flew,
Like lumberjacks served up a plate of tofu.

Up to the rooftop they carried the sleigh
(The holes in the shingles are there to this day).

Out bounded the man, who went straight to the flue.
I knew in an instant just what I should do.

After donning my slippers, downstairs did I dash
To see this trespasser emerge from the ash.

His clothes were all covered with soot, but of
    course,
From our wood-fueled alternative energy source.

Through the grime I distinguished the make of his
    duds—
He was dressed all in fur, fairly dripping with blood.

"We're a cruelty-free house!" I proclaimed with
    such heat
He was startled and tripped on the logs at his feet.

He stood back up dazed, but with mirth in
    his eyes.
It was then that I noticed his unhealthy size.

He was almost as wide as when standing erect,
A lover of fatty fried foods, I suspect.

But that wasn't all to make sane persuns choke:
In his teeth sat a pipe that was belching out smoke!

I could scarcely believe what invaded our house.
This carcinogenic and overweight louse

Was so red in the face from his energy spent,
I expected a heart attack right there and then.

Behind him he toted a red velvet bag
Full to exploding with sinister swag.

He asked, "Where is your tree?" with a face
    somewhat long.
I said, "Out in the yard, which is where it belongs."

"But where will I put all the presents I've brought?"
I looked at him squarely and said, "Take the lot

"To some frivolous people who think that they need
To succumb to the sickness of commerce and greed,

"Whose only joy comes from the act of consuming,
Thus sending the stock of the retailers booming."

He blinked and said, "Ho, ho, ho! But you're
    kidding."
I gave him a stare that was stern and forbidding.

"Surely children need something with which to have
    fun?
It's like childhood's over before it's begun."

He looked in my eyes for some sign of assent,
But I strengthened my will and refused to relent.

"They have plenty of fun," I cut to the gist,
"And your mindless distractions have never been
    missed.

"They take CPR so that they can save lives,
And go door-to-door for the used clothing drives.

"They recycle, renew, reuse—and reveal
For saving the planet a laudable zeal.

"When they padlock themselves to a fence to protest
Against nuclear power, we think they're the best."

He said, "But they're children—lo, when do they
    play?"
I countered, "Is that why you've driven your sleigh,

"To bring joy to the hearts of each child and tot?
All right, open your bag; let's see what you've
    got."

He sheepishly did as I'd asked and behold!
A Malibu Barbie in a skirt made of gold.

"You think that my girls will like playing with
    this,
An icon of sexist, consumerist kitsch?

"With its unnatural figure and airheaded grin,
This trollop makes every girl yearn to be thin,

"And take up fad diets and binging and purging
Instead of respecting her own body's urging

"To welcome the shape that her body has found
And rejoice to be lanky, short, skinny, or round."

Deep in his satchel he searched for a toy,
Saying, "This is a hit with most little boys."

And what did he put in my trembling hand
But a gun from the BrainBlasters Power Command!

"It's a 'hit,' to be sure," I sneered in his face,
"And a plague to infect the whole human race!

"How 'bout grenades or some working bazookas
To turn *all* of our kids into half-wit palookas?"

I seized on his bag just to see for myself
The filth being spread by this odious elf.

An Easy-Bake Oven—ah, goddess, what perfidy!
To hoodwink young girls into household captivity!

Plus an archery play set with shafts that fly out,
The very thing needed to put your eye out.

And toy metal tractors, steam shovels, and cranes
For tearing down woodlands and scarring the plains,

Plus "games" like Monopoly, Pay Day, Tycoon,
As if lessons in greed can't start up too soon.

And even more weapons from BrainBlasters Co.,
Like cannons and nunchucks and ray guns that glow.

That's all I could find in his red velvet sack—
Perverseness and mayhem to set us all back.

(But I did find one book that caused me to
ponder—
Some fine bedtime tales by a fellow named
Garner.)

"We need none of this," I announced in a huff,
"No 'business-as-usual' holiday stuff.

"We sow in our offspring more virtue than this.
Your 'toys' offer some things they never will
miss."

The big man's expression was a trifle bereaved
As he shouldered his pack and got ready to leave.

"I pity the kids who grow up around here,
Who're never permitted to be of good cheer,

202

"Who aren't allowed leisure for leisure's own sake,
But must fret every minute—it makes my heart
   break!"

"Enough histrionics! Don't pity our kids
If they don't do as Macy's or Toys 'R' Us bids.

"They live by their principles first and foremost
And know what's important," to him did I boast.

"Pray, could I meet them?" "Oh no, they're not here.
They're up on the roof, liberating your deer!"

Then Santa Claus sputtered and pointed his finger
But, mad as he was, he had no time to linger.

He flew up the chimney like smoke from a fire,
And up on the roof I heard voices get higher.

I ran outside the co-op to see him react
To my children's responsible, kindhearted act.

He chased them away, and disheartened, dismayed,
He rehitched his reindeer (who'd docilely stayed).

I watched with delight as he scooted off then.
He'd be too embarrassed to come back again.

But with parting disdain, do you know what he said,
When this overweight huckster took off in his sled?

This reindeer enslaver, this exploiter of elves?
"Happy Christmas to all, but get over yourselves!!"

FROSTY
THE PERSUN
OF SNOW

obby and Betty were two siblings who fought over everything. Sometimes they fought over big things, sometimes they fought over little things (and as with most male/female conflict communication patterns, they usually couldn't even agree on which issues were big and which were little). No amount of crisis intervention could get them to stop bickering.

One winter day, their frustrated caregiver sent them outside to play. A layer of fresh snow had fallen the previous night, the first of the season, and the world outside looked as heavily frosted as a matrimonial enslavement cake. As everything around them glistened, Bobby and Betty tried to agree on what games to play.

Should they make a snow fort? Too militaristic, said Betty.

How about snow angels? No, countered Bobby, they had been raised agnostic. Besides, such a public display of religious figures might make others uncomfortable.

And so it was with sledding, skating, and snowball fights—all were rejected for one reason or another. Then Betty suggested that they create people out of snow. Try as he might, Bobby couldn't find anything wrong in his sister's idea, so they each started to roll the biggest snowballs they could. Then they set these on top of each other for a body. Betty rolled a smaller snowball for a head and lifted it high atop the other two. They used two twigs to give it arms, and two lumps of coal and a button to give it a face. Bobby wanted to put a corncob pipe in its mouth, but Betty objected, saying the implied endorsement would harm the more impressionable children in the neighborhood.

Bobby said angrily, "When I make a snowman, he always has a corncob pipe!"

"What do you mean?" Betty answered. "This was my idea, and I say it's a snowwommon!"

"But it's *shaped* like a man!" said Bobby.

"Only to a phallocentric world view like yours!" said Betty.

"How can it be a wommon if we use the old top hat? Womyn don't wear top hats!"

"Oh yeah? What about Marlene Dietrich?"

And so it continued, with neither side budging an inch and the snow figure standing there, a silent witness. In a snit, Bobby decided to show his sibling that it was indeed a masculine snow individual, and slammed the hat on top of its head.

As soon as he did so, a quick gust of wind blew about them, and snow crystals spun around and around like a frigid tornado. Then, as suddenly as it had started, the wind settled down. Bobby and Betty wiped the snow from their eyes. They were about to resume their argument when an innocent voice asked, "What's all the fuss about?"

The siblings stopped and turned to the source of the voice. There, right where they had just assembled their frigid figure, stood a living, breathing, and fully articulate snow being! Their mouths fell open as they stared at this marvel.

"It seems like such a silly argument," it continued, "especially since you neglected to give me any private parts."

Betty regained her composure quickly. "I don't care if you *were* born only an instant ago," she said. "How can you be so naive as to think a persun's gender is determined by their physical equipment? It's a cultural issue first and foremost."

"If you want to get huffy," retorted the newcomer, "tell me why you were going to assign me a gender without asking me my preference first."

Betty's face reddened at her insensitivity.

"So what would you prefer?" asked Bobby.

"After watching the way you two communicate, I prefer neither. I think I'd like to be called a 'persun of snow.'"

"And what should your name be?" asked Betty, trying to make amends.

"In a post-modern comment on the preconceptions of society at large, I'm going to choose the most obvious name possible. You can call me 'Frosty'!"

Bobby and Betty agreed that it was a wonderful name. The arrival of their new friend was so magickal and exciting that the children completely forgot their earlier argument. Frosty and the pre-adults danced and played and laughed together for hours, with nary a cross word between the siblings.

As the sun climbed in the sky, the children continued to scamper about, but Frosty began to feel wet and heavy. Soon the persun of snow was having a difficult time keeping up with the pre-adults.

"What's the matter, Frosty?" they asked with concern.

"Oh, it's so hot!" Frosty said. "I'm not made of flesh and blood like you. If the temperature keeps rising, soon there will be nothing left of me."

"The Earth's getting warmer, due to the depletion of the ozone layer," said Bobby matter-of-factly. "We learned all about it at Montessori school."

"The ozone layer?" repeated Frosty. "I don't know what that is, but we better do something about it fast, or I'll turn into a puddle of water."

"How about a march on Washington?" suggested Betty.

"Yes, that's exactly the thing!" said her brother.

"Then let's hurry," said Frosty. "If enough of us march, the government will *have* to take action."

Frosty ran through the neighborhood, mobilizing the rest of the snow citizens. In backyards and front yards, in parks and in playgrounds, snow persuns of every size and shape listened to Frosty's plan. The magick from its top hat and the passion in its speech enabled them all to throw off the icy chains of passivity and take positive action for their own survival. Soon the charismatic Frosty had gathered a good-sized crowd, ready to take their argument to the government.

Bobby and Betty did their part as well. They rounded up their dog Spot and their kitty Puff and prepared to head off. Then they called their friends Ahmout and Fatima, and their friends Ho-shi and Chin-wa, and their friends Shadrach and Lu'Minaria, and their friend Heather and her two mommies, and the whole crowd joined in with the march of the persuns of snow.

Frosty walked at the head of the parade, holding a broomstick high. Others carried signs with messages like "No Ozone = No-Snow Zone" and "We Won't Just Melt Away!" En route to Washington, they picked up other supporters, snow and non-snow alike. Frosty and friends also got the attention of the media, since the sight of the Rubenesque, dark-eyed snowpersuns made such "great TV" for the video crews.

Soon the marchers made it to the Capitol Mall, where they were determined to camp until the president agreed to meet and hear their concerns. Where the icy protestors gathered, the mall looked as if it were covered with a plush white carpet, with tiny clusters of humans tossed on it like colorful stones. Unfortunately, Washington did not have a cool climate at all, and many of the persuns of snow were beginning to feel very uncomfortable.

It wasn't long before the news finally came: The vice president had agreed to speak with Frosty on television, in a remote one-on-one discussion about the steps needed to halt ozone breakdown. Excitement rippled through the encampment on the mall. Finally their concerns would be taken seriously!

A camera crew came later that day and set up the chairs, monitors, and cameras that would be needed. Bobby and Betty were particularly excited for Frosty, who was by now a dear friend. Ever since Frosty's arrival, in fact, the children had scarcely quarreled at all. Betty hugged Frosty around the neck and said, "We're so proud of you!"

"Aw, thanks," said Frosty, "but I haven't done

much of anything yet. You should be proud of how everyone got together—snow and skin alike—and worked to protect the environment. Now please listen carefully. If anything should ever happen to me, I hope you two will be able to stop fighting once and for all and lead the movement in my place."

Bobby and Betty promised their friend to do their best.

It was time for the broadcast to begin. The TV people tried to put some makeup on Frosty, to cut down on the glare off its forehead, but soon realized the task was impossible. Frosty sat in the appointed chair and waited for the director's signal.

Suddenly the lights went on and the sign was given that they were on the air. Out of respect for the office, Frosty let the vice president give the opening remarks. As the politician talked, the persun of snow began to feel very warm and sluggish. When the vice president was through, Frosty tried to state the marchers' position firmly, but the persun of snow was feeling so tired that it paused often and had trouble catching its breath. As time went on, Frosty slumped in the chair, looking worse and worse. By the time Bobby and Betty screamed, "Stop! Turn off the lights!" it was too late. On national television, under the glare of the hot lights, Frosty had melted irrevocably into a gray pile of slush.

Bobby and Betty were very sad for their friend, as were the rest of the protestors. But in the end, its demise was not tragic at all. Frosty had dramatized the plight of the ozone layer in a way that a squadron of scientists could never have. Everyone watching television that day was deeply moved by Frosty's brave sacrifice. Switchboards at the White House and the Capitol were lit up for hours, and within weeks new guidelines were established for both industry and government agencies to reduce the emissions that were eating away at the ozone.

Bobby and Betty took Frosty's top hat and went home. They tried to do as Frosty said and stop squabbling, but without their friend's calming influence, it was very hard for them. Their very different ideas about how to honor Frosty's memory and keep the movement alive couldn't be reconciled. As the weather got warmer, they moved on to other arguments and began to forget about their wintry friend. The next year, when they tried to recapture the magick of that first snowfall, they were unable to find Frosty's top hat and had to settle for making persuns of snow who faced their fates silently and unflinchingly.

THE NUTCRACKER

nce, many Christmas Eves ago, Clara's parents were throwing a party for their many friends and relations. These festive gatherings were an annual event in Clara's household, a singular opportunity during the year for everyone to forget their cares, to dance and gossip, and to eat as many fatty and sugary foods as possible. (Clara's parents felt it best to get such impulses out of one's system on a regular basis.) For the children, the chef would always bake a large gingerbread castle, wonderfully decorated with scores of marzipan peasants and serfs scaling the walls and overthrowing the parasitical king and his family.

These parties were always a joy for Clara and her brother Fritz because they meant presents, especially presents from their Uncle Drosselmeier. Their uncle was a mysterious, out-of-the-mainstream sort of chap, whose alternative lifestyle (if indeed he even had a lifestyle) was the subject of much speculation. He was gaunt of face and wore a gargantuan powdered wig and a patch over one eye ("Mostly for effect," said Clara's father). He was predisposed dramatic gestures and exotic, ostentatious clothing—anything to shake up people's bourgeois complacency. But Clara and Fritz loved their charismatic relative, both for his independent attitude and for the marvelously intricate mechanical toys he built for them.

On this Christmas Eve, their uncle arrived later than usual, but the delay merely heightened the excitement of his arrival. It wasn't until after the guests had gorged themselves on dinner that he finally appeared in the main hall with a sack over his shoulder. Clara, Fritz, and the other children could barely contain their delight, and nearly knocked Uncle Drosselmeier down to see what he'd brought this year.

Their uncle snickered cryptically, then reached into his bag with a great flourish. The adults as well as the pre-adults gathered round him in curiosity.

The man of augmented eccentricity smiled at all the attention and pulled out a silver top, decorated with intriguing symbols.

"To make holiday gift-giving more inclusive and outreaching," he said in a quavery voice, "I have developed this, the world's first automatic dreidel." He set this marvel on the tabletop, where it began to spin on its own power, glittering and gleaming and whirring. When it finally began to slow down and fell on its side, it made a strange clicking sound, then spit coins out of a small slit near its handle.

Everyone gasped and clapped their hands at this mechanical wonder, except for a few spoilsports who complained that children were forgetting how to entertain themselves with all these new automatic playthings. Next from his satchel Uncle Drossel-meier pulled out a doll, which looked ordinary enough after the spectacular dreidel. He smirked at everyone's apparent disappointment, then turned a knob in the doll's back. "Momma . . . " said the doll in a natural-sounding voice, "or Poppa . . . which-ever caregiver is available."

The crowd thought this was quite ingenious and also socially progressive. He presented the doll to his niece, who handled it gingerly. Then from the bag, he pulled out the final gift: a hand-carved Nutcracker, dressed as a soldier and wearing the most comical expression. He handed this little figure to Fritz.

Oh, was there a hue and cry at this! It was bad enough to reinforce gender roles by handing Clara the doll, but on top of that, to give young, impressionable Fritz such an obvious symbol of castration and emasculation was inexcusable! People grew so angry that Uncle Drosselmeier feared he would be forcibly ejected from the party.

"I intended no harm," he protested sincerely. "I meant for the children to share the toys equally." He then swapped the doll and the Nutcracker between Clara and Fritz. (Years later, this incident, among others, would come back to Fritz while he underwent repressed-memory therapy, much to the chagrin and legal entanglement of his well-meaning uncle.)

Clara liked the Nutcracker and played with it for the rest of the evening. The guests ate and drank long into the night, giving not a thought to the purging and colonic irrigation that would be necessary the next morning. After they had all left, Clara's father tried to persuade her it was time for bed.

"Please may I stay up a while longer?" she asked. "The Nutcracker is telling me stories about why he left the military."

Her father smiled wearily and walked upstairs. Some time later, Clara set the Nutcracker on the cupboard shelf just as the clock struck midnight. As the final chime rang, very strange things began to happen in the room. Through the floor and out of the baseboards came a crowd of squeaking, scurrying mice—hundreds of mice, an entire army of mice! And in their midst stood their leader, a multi-craniumed Mouse King, who wore a golden crown on each of his seven heads.

Clara was marvelling at this when she heard the toys in the cupboard begin to stir and shout. "Oh, help," they cried. "The Mouse King and his expansionist forces have returned! Oh, save us, Nutcracker! Lead us into battle!"

To Clara's utter amazement, her little friend the Nutcracker walked forward and addressed them all: "Good citizens, think for a minute. Do you really want to perpetuate the old 'Great Man' myth of history/herstory? Important actions arise from the will of the people, not from the megalomania of any one individual!"

The toys admitted that their first impulse had been a tad servile and reactionary. They formed a committee to examine possible action plans to counter the Mouse King's advances. They then appointed the Nutcracker to head a fact-finding and cultural-interchange team to develop a dialog with the mice.

The fact-finding team headed out and returned twenty minutes later, tattered and bloodied. The toys then voted to assemble a crisis intervention team, again with the Nutcracker at the helm. This team headed out and returned fifteen minutes later, in even worse shape than the first. It seemed their non-aggressive options were dwindling.

After much debate, the toys agreed on their final course of action: They would send out a team of mediators to negotiate a peaceful settlement to the current crisis. Despite his now-tattered appearance, the Nutcracker was again chosen to lead the delegation. With the blessings and hopes of the other toys and Clara, the team went forth. Twenty minutes passed with no word, then an hour, then ninety minutes. Finally, after two anxious hours, the mediators returned with joyful news.

"We have an agreement with the Mouse King," announced the Nutcracker. "If we will help them liberate food from the pantry regularly, they will retreat from the territory they currently occupy." The toys let out a cheer and hailed the mediation team for their wisdom and hard work.

The Nutcracker walked over to Clara, who had stayed to lend her support to the beleaguered toys. "The Mouse King wasn't nearly so dangerous and irrational as he seemed," explained the wooden individual. "I finally deduced from his seven-headed appearance that he might be suffering from some sort of multiple-persunality disorder, which made him delusional and paranoid. Once I made contact with the most rational and judicious of his persunalities, we easily reached an accord."

"Bravo!" cried Clara. "Your dedication is to be praised. Mice certainly have been feared and marginalized for much too long."

The Nutcracker made a mannerly bow. "And now, sweet Clara, I would like to take you on a journey to my own kingdom, through the Christmas Wood and the Glade of the Sugar Plum Fairies, to the capital of Toyland, the wondrous Candytown!"

Clara was surprised by his offer. "I-I'm sorry," she stammered, "but . . . no."

The Nutcracker was crestfallen, and his larger-than-average jaw dropped to his chest.

"You see, we've been discussing just this sort of idea in our Storybook Womyn's Study Group," explained Clara. "We object that it's always the young womyn who are forced to undertake these disruptive journeys. The obvious implication is that we are all docile, helpless, and easily manipulated, and that our backgrounds and identities are of lesser importance. And even you should be able to see how such a journey is symbolic of the violent abduction that occurs on the wedding night. So, in memory of Dorothy and of Alice—poor, poor Alice; she's never regained her grip on reality, you know—I have to decline."

The Nutcracker felt a bit foolish after this. Unaware of the symbolism of his invitation, he certainly had intended no disrespect. He excused himself in the most courteous manner and gathered all the toys together again in the cupboard. The last thing Clara remembered before waking up was the Nutcracker's courtly bow, which she accepted with the graciousness with which it was offered.

The next morning, Clara found herself curled up on the floor of the drawing room, next to the toy cupboard. Inside she could see all the toys in their usual places, and in the middle of them all, the Nutcracker—immobile, steadfast, and still smiling. "What a wonderful, peace-loving dream!" she said to herself. "Yet not so much a dream as an attainable reality."

Clara stretched and rose from the carpet. As she looked around the room in the early morning light, her happiness was tempered by a pitiful scene. On the table in the dining room sat the ruins of the gingerbread castle, which had been sacked and destroyed by mice while she dreamt during the night.

RUDOLPH
THE NASALLY
EMPOWERED
REINDEER

he story of Rudolph is a familiar one to most of the pre-adults in America and other parts of the Western world (not that this fact is an endorsement of Western culture, just an acknowledgment that the publicity and merchandising machines run more efficiently in those areas). While the image of an eager young reindeer cheerfully giving his all for

Santa Claus might be useful to department stores and jingle writers, the truth of his story is more complicated.

It's true that from birth Rudolph was a unique individual, that his luminescent olfactory organ made him different from (but not inferior to) the other reindeer in his age category, and that they often maliciously taunted him about his supra-nasal capabilities. Some reindeer caregivers, concerned that his nose had resulted from radioactive fallout or was somehow contagious, warned their fawns not to play with him.

What is *not* true is that Rudolph was disappointed to be so ostracized. While his parents successfully fought to have him schooled alongside the other young bucks and does, Rudolph always fancied himself an outsider. In fact, he worked to cultivate his image as an "angry young reindeer." He had no interest in the other reindeer and their inane games. He took himself and his fluorescent gift seriously and was convinced he had a higher calling in this life: to improve the fortunes of the working reindeer and overthrow the oppressive tyranny of Santa Claus.

For untold years, the success of Santa's toy-making monopoly depended on the co-option and exploitation of both the reindeer and elf populations. To this end, his most important criteria for the reindeer in his team were strong legs, a ten-point rack, and minimal gray matter. (The fact that he only recruited bucks for his team and excluded the does is cause for more outrage—Santa insisted it was to protect the morale of the enlisted bucks—but unfortunately, in Rudolph's time, the does were still awaiting their liberatrix.)

To Santa, Rudolph was one of the Northland's most dangerous creatures: a reindeer with a brain. He had seen a few during his years at the Pole, but there was something about Rudolph that made him especially nervous. It might have been the deer's standoffish attitude, or the rumors that he was organizing meetings with the other reindeer late at night. Santa also sensed a charisma in Rudolph that, if not kept in proper check, might disrupt his tidy little enterprise.

And so it was that, on that fabled foggy evening, Santa found himself in a bind. Harsh weather conditions left him unable to exploit the aerodynamic talents of his team. He had of course flown them through all sorts of dangerous weather before, with no thought to the deer's physical strain or mental trauma. But on this night the weather was so tempestuous that the bearded slave driver was fearful for his own safety and for the insurance headaches that a crash at his own toy works would certainly create.

Although Santa had known for years about Rudolph's gift for incandescent dissemination, he had not called special attention to it. In due time, Santa selfishly calculated, a use for it would arise, and until then there was no need to tip off how valuable Rudolph's skill might prove to be. That moment had finally arrived. On that foggy night, he sought out Rudolph among the herd and, wearing his humblest and most pleading face, asked him, "Rudolph, with your nose so bright, won't you guide my sleigh tonight?"

The young reindeer looked him over carefully. After a few moments of silence, he said, "No."

Santa blinked a few times and repeated, "No?" The herd could scarcely believe its ears as well.

"No. Not without concessions," replied the creature who happened to be antlered. "The days when we jump every time you whistle are over."

"What are you talking about, concessions?" blustered Santa, who hadn't planned on this twist. "This is your big break, your chance to join the team. This is the life's dream of every young reindeer."

Rudolph laughed. "This is starting to sound like *A Star Is Born*. Next you're going to tell me, 'Kid, you're going out there a nervous young buck, but you're coming back . . . a star.'"

The herd all chuckled at this remark. Perhaps such a gung-ho speech was all too familiar to them. Santa reddened, realizing he'd made a tactical error in approaching this young firebrand in public. He said, "It's cold out here. Why don't we talk this over inside my chalet. I have some very good moss and lichens, just picked . . . "

"I'll eat what everyone else eats," countered Rudolph, "and whatever you have to say to me, you can say out here." The other reindeer were watching this face-off with great interest. For years, they had treated Rudolph with suspicion for all his bold ideas, but now he was bravely sticking up for them at the expense of his own career. Some shouted encouragement, while the more reactionary deer grumbled about not rocking the kayak.

Santa began to feel some pressure as the minutes ticked away and the fog grew thicker. Finally he asked Rudolph what his demands were.

"You work the reindeer too hard, with no consideration for our families," Rudolph said. "We want a guarantee of no work on holidays."

For the next thirty minutes Santa tried to explain the disadvantages of this idea, the main one being, of course, that the reindeer only worked one night a year anyway, and since that night *always* fell on a holiday, such a change would make their jobs (and his) rather difficult to fulfill. Rudolph eventually agreed to table the issue for the time being.

Checking his watch, Santa was starting to sweat, even in the Arctic cold. "Could we speed this up?" he asked. "Or maybe forge a temporary working agreement that we can make permanent after Christmas?"

Rudolph snorted in his face. "We weren't born yesterday, Claus. No contract, no flight. If Christmas doesn't come this year, who do you think the children will blame? The reindeer? The weather? The Interstate Commerce Commission? No, they'll blame the overfed guy in the red suit."

Santa imagined the public relations headaches this would cause him, and his frame began to sag. Rudolph grilled him on such issues as health care, paternity leave, profit sharing, and joint decision-making councils. As the fog refused to lift and the minutes ticked away, Santa granted more and more of the deer's demands.

In the end, Rudolph and the reindeer rank-and-file could claim a number of victories: The deer would be required to fly only one night a year, and after four hours on the job, they would receive a ninety-minute dinner break and three fifteen-minute breaks. Santa was required to keep four alternate reindeer on standby for the duration of Christmas Eve at full pay and benefits. In addition, the mandatory retirement age was lowered to eight years, after which the reindeer were to receive a full pension and lifetime health care.

After all the terms were finalized, an exhausted but relieved Santa Claus hitched Rudolph up with the rest of the team. The other deer gave Rudolph three cheers for standing up for their rights against "the man," which the nasally empowered reindeer, feeling fulfilled for the first time, gratefully accepted. Using his unique luminescent gift, he led the sleigh through the inhospitable weather and Christmas that year was saved.

EPILOGUE

Like the fabled prophet in his own land, however, Rudolph found his real influence evaporating soon after that. For weeks he was praised by all the other reindeer, who told him, "You'll go down in history/herstory!" All the attention and admiration, however, began to feel superficial and distracting. Rudolph felt that any lionization of him would take energy away from the continuing fight for the well-being of the working reindeer. In a facile attempt to emulate their new hero, the other young reindeer began to wear bright red coverings on their noses. When Rudolph expressed his displeasure with this, some muttered that he was becoming too humorless and doctrinaire.

To Rudolph, this first agreement with Santa was to be just the beginning. He envisioned the eventual creation of a working reindeer's paradise, a toy-making and distribution collective where the means of production were shared by everyone. Unfortunately, many of the other reindeer began to take their newly won benefits as their inviolable right, bestowed by nature. They grew fat on too much moss and complained that their improved work schedules were still too taxing. Factions began to form among them about the best ways to invest their new pension fund. Rudolph tried to convince the dissident deer that they needed to stand united, but they began to resent his holier-than-thou attitude.

Some spread the rumor that he was an agent provocateur, sent by other aeronautically gifted animals seeking to gain Santa's favor and put the deer out of their jobs. While such theories were patently absurd, they served to discredit Rudolph and embolden his detractors. Eventually, he was voted out of the union he had helped establish. After this indignity, Rudolph decided to strike off for Lapland, where he felt the undomesticated reindeer were more in control of their own future.

And so, like other revolutionaries before him, Rudolph the angry young reindeer lived out the rest of his days in exile, bitterly wondering how a movement with such promise could prove to be so fragile in the end.

A CHRISTMAS CAROL

STAVE I—MARLEY'S POST-LIFE REPRESENTATIVE

 arley was non-viable, to begin with; there is no doubt whatever about that, except for general philosophical questions about the permanence of death and the very real possibilities of reincarnation. The label "non-viable" is also fairly confining, yet, as Marley left no heirs or significant others, protests were not forthcoming. With his karma in the condition it was, chances were good that the host body that Marley's spirit might next inhabit would be of the

invertebrate type, and until a champion for those speechless phyla comes forward, it is unlikely we shall ever hear from or about Marley again. So, for all practical purposes, Marley was as non-viable as a doornail. Unless you happen to be an animist, of course. But enough digression.

Scrooge certainly knew Marley had advanced into a post-life situation. The two had been business partners for many years, in a ruthless capitalistic operation that took advantage of people's caffeine addictions and exploited coffee farmers in developing nations. The business had started with good and generous intentions, and even offered stock options to the coffee farmers at one time, but these efforts had eroded over many years of competition and rapt attention to the bottom line. All that was left of their original egalitarian vision was a string of chrome-and-marble-filled coffee bars and a relaxed company dress code. While Marley was partly responsible for this reactionary shift, the real architect of this venal situation was his still-living partner.

Oh! But a tight-fisted hand at the grindstone was Scrooge! A squeezing, wrenching, grasping, scraping, clutching, covetous old sinner! And, as you might well imagine, this did nothing for his self-esteem. Oh, how long and wearisome life can be when hampered by a negative self-image!

Once upon a time—of all the good days in the year, on Christmas Eve (not to slight the importance of any day held holy by adherents of any other religion or non-religion, or of any other day not so designated)—Scrooge sat in his warehouse office, poring over the week's spreadsheets. It was cold, bleak, biting weather. The stock exchanges had only just closed, but outside it was quite dark already.

The door to Scrooge's office was kept open that he might keep an eye on his employees—of which there was now only one. The rest had been released just the previous week in the latest right-sizing of Scrooge & Marley, Inc. While these decruits had been released at an inauspicious time of year, Scrooge liked to think he had done them a favor by allowing them to pursue their own entrepreneurial interests. "Besides," thought he, "the taxes I've paid over the years have made unemployment benefits plenty attractive. These people are practically on Easy Street already."

Through the door Scrooge could see his lone administrative assistant, Roberto "Bob" Cratchit, busily inputting sales data. Poor Cratchit could almost see his breath, the temperature in the warehouse was kept so low. Scrooge led an ascetic lifestyle himself and expected others to do the same. He believed that excess heat and comfort sapped the human spirit and made the body susceptible to numerous diseases. And while his stated intents were to promote vitality and conserve fossil fuels, in his heart of hearts Scrooge more greatly relished the monetary savings of such an icy atmosphere. He kept the thermostat under lock and key in his office, so his staff of one was forced to make do with heavy coats, thick socks, and plenty of hot miso soup brought from home.

For you see, money was Scrooge's sole interest now, and only love. His life had not always been thus. As a youth, he was active in many progressive, humanitarian movements, mainly because he felt it was a good way to meet womyn. But he never in his life embraced himself as a worthwhile persun, and soon he began to distrust others as much as he distrusted himself. In his insecurity, he found comfort in accumulating wealth, since his money would never break his heart or ask to borrow his car. Such displaced affection would be merely sad in his isolated case, were it not so tragically prevalent in the world at large.

"A merry, non-sectarian Christmas, Uncle!" cried a cheerful voice. It was Scrooge's nephew, Fred, who had managed to sneak up on Scrooge and Cratchit.

"Bah!" said Scrooge. "Humbug!"

"Christmas a humbug, Uncle!" exclaimed Fred, whose cheerful face was quite ruddy from the cold. "You don't mean that, I am sure?"

"Yes," said Scrooge, "a humbug!" and swatted at his desk with a ledger. When he lifted the book, there sat the pasty remains of a rare Honduran humming cockroach.

"Uncle, how cruel!"

"We get these frequently with the bean shipments," replied Scrooge. "If I were to leave them alone, our interior environment would be overrun, so save your Rachel Carson act for someplace else. Now, what's all this hogwash about a merry Christmas? Mighty presumptuous of you."

"Then I amend it to 'Happy holidays.'"

"Still presumptuous."

"'Greetings of the season'?"

"Bah!" said Scrooge angrily. "I'm weary of this 'season' and all its forced gaiety. What is this season but the chance to feel another year older and not any more persunally fulfilled? A time to juggle the books for the end of the tax year? An opportunity to be labelled unpatriotic if you don't splurge on enough baubles to buy your way into people's affections? If I could work my will, every idiot who spouts a 'Season's greetings' would be made to watch 'The Osmond Family Christmas Special' for a solid month and be force-fed 100 McDonald's eggnog shakes!"

"Uncle, you can't mean that."

"I can and do! And don't denigrate my opinions, Nephew! What good has this oppressive holiday ever done you?"

"Since you ask," replied Fred, "the holidays give me a chance to keep up appearances and assuage my middle-class guilt, so that I can drop a check in the mail and think I've done more than my share to better the world. It's a time when I'm told that everyone opens their hearts to the good in their fellow persuns, when rich and poor alike can drink in its kindness, delaying all-out class warfare for another year. So even if the holidays only reward me in trickle-down economic benefits and a warm fuzzy feeling, I should like to say I'm pretty much in favor of them, generally."

"Right on!" said Bob Cratchit.

"Enough from you!" Scrooge warned his staff.

"I'm surrounded by the cerebrally undercapitalized! What right have you to be merry? You're overextended enough."

"What right have you to be morose?" retorted his nephew. "Your catalog sales are big enough. I came to invite you over to our house tomorrow. My wife and I are having some people over, a little wine and cheese—strictly casual."

"Bah! I'd rather switch to decaf."

"We'll be playing Scattergories," coaxed his nephew.

"Good afternoon," said Scrooge.

"Then I'll just wish you enhanced seasonal benefits and a nurturing new year."

"Good afternoon!" said Scrooge.

His nephew left without an angry word, notwithstanding, and bestowed greetings of the season on Scrooge's assistant, who returned them gratefully.

Scrooge's phone rang, and he picked up the receiver to hear a chipper recorded voice say, "Happy holidays! . . . You have been selected to receive a wonderful free gift . . . of a lovely fruitcake and at the same time . . . help an organization working to better our community. To find out how to take advantage of this exciting offer . . . please remain on the line . . ."

Scrooge slammed down the receiver bitterly. "Humbug!" he muttered, and swatted another roach on his desk.

When five o'clock finally arrived, Roberto Cratchit cleared off his desk and prepared to leave. Scrooge strode over with a glowering look and said to his sole employee, "You'll want the entire day off tomorrow, I suppose?"

"We've been through this over and over," said Roberto. "If you really want someone here with you tomorrow, call a temp agency. If you want me here, you'll have to pay triple-time for the legal holiday, like my contract says."

Scrooge scoffed, "Bah! What could be 'legal' about picking a businessman's pocket in such a way? You just be careful to respect your body tomorrow and don't be hung over when you come in the day after."

Not in a mood to argue, Bob agreed to keep his excesses to a moderate level and left the warehouse. Scrooge stayed to work a few more hours, then turned off his lights and closed up. In the parking lot, he braced himself against the cold and climbed into his banged-up, well-traveled Volvo sedan. He could certainly have afforded a newer car, but the

Volvo's resale value had precipitously sunk and Scrooge wouldn't part with it for such a small figure. So determined was he to squeeze every last dime of value from the car that he didn't realize that the rear bumper was still attached only by the myriad bumper stickers that adorned it—bumper stickers for numerous worthy causes that were sadly stuck in mute testimony to the man's youthful idealism.

Scrooge soon reached his home, which stood at the far end of a nearly vacant condominium complex of renovated industrial buildings. He parked the Volvo near the main entrance and hurriedly opened the courtyard gate. Crossing the grim, unadorned cloister to his own door, he saw none of his neighbors, which suited him perfectly. Yet somehow he didn't feel alone.

He unlocked his front door, climbed the stairs, and entered his condo on the third floor. If this had ever been a welcoming domain, there was no trace of it now. The lights were kept perpetually dim, and to call the furnishings spartan would have been an insult to the inhabitants of that noble and ancient land. Scrooge thought that this sparseness imparted a certain air of Oriental spirituality to the place, but to a visitor (if Scrooge had ever had one) it merely looked cheap and underfurnished. From his entryway, he noticed that, for the first time in memory, the message light on his answering machine was blinking. Assuming it was another phone solicitation, he thought of ignoring it, yet the insistent red flashes caused him unease. With a hesitant motion, he pushed the playback button and heard what he thought was the voice of his terminally inconvenienced partner, Jacob Marley, in a mournful intonation. "Sssssscrrooooooooggge!" * *beep* *

Scrooge slapped at the machine, annoyed by the seeming prank. "Bah!" he said, "I don't believe it!" and went into the kitchen. Recently he had read about the health benefits of a strict diet of watery gruel, and he had adopted this bleak and frugal regimen. He served up a bowl of the gruel (unheated, of course), took it into the living room, and settled into a cushion on the floor to eat. But no sooner had he done so than he heard an unearthly clattering in the courtyard. Scrooge stopped eating and listened. A sound arose like chains and heavy equipment being dragged over the trash cans. He made a mental note to talk to the condo board about extra security and double-bolted his door.

Scrooge jumped with a start at the next crash, which sounded like the door to his building being kicked in. He heard the clamor more loudly on the floors below, then coming up the stairs, then coming straight for his door.

"I still don't believe it," attested Scrooge.

But the blood drained from his face when the source of the noise pushed itself through his door. It was the post-life representative of Jacob Marley! The spirit was dressed in the jogging suit and expensive sneakers Marley favored in life, now worn and tattered from the grave. Around its head it wore a sweatband, but curiously under its chin rather than across its brow. The horrible clanking sounds Scrooge had heard came from a chain it carried that was fastened around its waist. The chain was made, Scrooge noticed, of barbells, abdominal exercisers, and random parts from broken Soloflex systems.

"Still working to feel the burn, eh, Jacob?" joked Scrooge uneasily.

"You don't believe in me?" asked the spectral visitor.

Scrooge said, "Usually I never question another's claims of spirituality, but I'm sorry, most people aren't so hammy about it." He tried to sound brave but wasn't very convincing.

"Why do you doubt your senses?" it asked.

"So now you're saying I should *believe* my senses?" asked a quick-thinking Scrooge, who often resorted to double-talk in sticky situations. "How limiting. Since when did Jacob Marley become a mere rationalist? Besides, if I were to believe my senses, it would look like I'm being haunted by the ghost of Jack La Lanne."

At this, the spirit raised a frightful cry and shook its chain with such a dismal and appalling noise that Scrooge clung tightly to his cushion in fear and fell over like a child's toy. But how much greater was the horror when the phantom removed the sweatband from around its head: Its jaw abruptly fell open and its teeth dropped out.

Scrooge got up on his knees, trembling. "Jacob, please," he begged. "Why have you come here? To show me false teeth?"

"That's just to start," said the non-corporeal visitor through its gums. "Do you know what else was false about me? Pectoral implants, calf implants, a hair weave, plastic surgery upon plastic surgery, even tinted contact lenses. Now in death I cannot tell which parts of me were original and which were paid for by installment. And because of this falsity, I am condemned to wander the world and witness those things which are genuine and true but in which I cannot share." Again the ghost let out a terrible cry. "I can never again visit southern California!"

Scrooge trembled and asked why he was fettered. "I wear the chain I forged in life," was the reply. "Each time I concentrated on the prefabricated and the superficial instead of the good and the true, I added another link to it. Do you realize the length of your own chain? It was this long seven years ago, and you have been working hard at it since."

"Have you no comfort to give me?" asked Scrooge.

"None. I know of your greed and your dual-visaged dealings. You value profits more than people, all in the name of some claptrap about the 'wisdom of the market' and 'a rising tide lifting all boats.' Such vanity! You know nothing about genuine worth, about what is truly valuable. Unless you mend your ways, you will receive a punishment worse than mine. My time here is nearly gone. I'm here to warn you that you still have a chance to escape my fate."

"You were always a good friend to me, Jacob," said Scrooge. "A good and dear friend, who knew me better than I knew myself. May I take this opportunity to thank you for—"

"Enough of your sucking up!" the specter interrupted. "You can't talk your way out of this. You will
be haunted this night by three extra-dimensional
intercessors."

"Angels?" asked Scrooge brightly.

"Nothing so trendy. Expect the first when the
clock strikes one."

"Can't I take them all at once," hinted Scrooge,
"and get it over with?"

"They are individual spirits," answered Marley's
shade, "each with different needs that must be
respected. You'd do well to remember that." When it
had said these words, the spirit picked up its teeth
and bound its head again. It walked backward from
Scrooge, and at every step Marley's post-life representative took, the window raised itself a little and
was soon completely open. The spirit then floated
out into the dark night with a mournful howl, and
the window slammed fast.

Scrooge examined his door, which was still
double-bolted. He tried to say "Humbug" but found
himself vocally incapacitated. Whether it was the

ordeal he had just experienced or the effect of the white-noise machine in the background, he crawled to his tatami mat in the bedroom and immediately fell asleep.

STAVE II—THE FIRST OF THE THREE
SPIRITUAL FACILITATORS

t was still dark when Scrooge next awoke. Lying on his mat, he laughed to himself for what he believed had happened earlier. While he remained open to the possibility of extra-scientific phenomena, he couldn't validate the previous evening's event as anything credible. Marley's image had been so melodramatic, after all, not to mention self-righteous and accusatory. Additionally, an all-gruel diet was known to have some side effects, one of which was vivid hallucinations.

Just then the alarm on his wristwatch beeped once, and instantly a bright light pierced the darkness of his room. When his eyes adjusted, Scrooge saw before him a strange figure—a being not quite adult in stature, yet not quite child-like in appearance. Its hair, which was stylishly blown and brushed, was silver as if from experience, and yet the puckish face had not a wrinkle on it, as nearly as Scrooge could tell through its makeup. It wore a radiant sport coat with a boutonniere of holly. But the strangest thing about it was that from behind its head, there sprung a bright light—actually an entire bank of lights from the camera crew that it had brought along with it.

"Who and what are you?" demanded Scrooge, trying to sound brave.

"I am the Spirit whose coming was foretold to you," it said into its microphone. "I am the Ghost of Christmas Retrospective, and this is my crew."

Scrooge asked the Spirit why it had brought all the cameras.

The Spirit said, "Nobody is really afraid of ghosts anymore. They all think I'm some sort of hologram or special effect. But come in with a hard-bitten, exposé-hungry camera crew, and you get people's attention."

"And what is it you want from me?"

"There are allegations that your life has been spent worshiping false idols and turning your back on the rest of persunkind. Would you care to comment on that?" The Spirit stuck its microphone in Scrooge's face.

He smiled smugly. "You must really take me for someone of overtaxed mental and emotional resources. I don't respond to anonymous allegations."

"Then you are telling us that you are the model of a concerned, conscientious, upright citizen?"

"Yes," Scrooge asserted, and added another untruth, "although definitely not wedded to the established order of things."

"Then we must have been mistaken," said the Spirit with a straight face. "I smell another story here. What do you say we review with you some of the events that shaped the upstanding man you are today?"

Scrooge saw nothing wrong with this and readily agreed. The Spirit had him sign a release then led him over to the window. "Wait a minute," said Scrooge. "We're three floors up. I'll fall."

"Give but a touch to my microphone cord," said the Spirit, "and you'll be borne aloft. But strap on this safety helmet anyway; I don't need any more lawsuits. And . . . we're rolling."

As these words were spoken, Scrooge, the Spirit, and the camera crew passed through the wall and suddenly found themselves in the midst of bedlam. A horde of people in gaudy and disheveled clothing surged and careened around them, while disco music pulsed loudly and incessantly. Amid laughter and occasional howling, men and womyn were telling persunal secrets, hidden desires, and undecorous jokes with an incredible amount of informality. But it apparently was all in excellent fun, at least by that era's standards. In this elegant, crowded hotel ballroom, the holiday cheer spilled as much from the hearts of the celebrants as out of the numerous glasses held aloft.

"And where are we now?" the Spirit asked as he shoved the mike in Scrooge's face.

Scrooge yelled over the din, "My gosh! This is one of the office parties that old Fezziwig used to throw, before the feds got him. It's good to see it all again—it was so hard to remember the morning after."

Scrooge recognized many old friends and acquaintances amidst the faces assembled there. He shouted out their names in recognition, but they paid him no mind, as was their prerogative as shades of the past. These slights worried Scrooge not a bit as he was swept up in a wave of nostalgia and festivity. He quite forgot himself amid all the merry-making and tried to join a "Soul Train" line. The Spirit and its crew watched bemusedly, feeling no obligation to stop him from his frivolity. The release they'd made him sign clearly stated that these were merely images of the past that would not be aware of his presence.

As the shades continued to eat, drink, and celebrate each others' company, the Spirit asked pointedly, "In your opinion, was Fezziwig misusing corporate assets, as the indictments charged?"

"Misusing? Not at all!" replied Scrooge. "Fezziwig was a great man, and a wonderful employer."

"But he allegedly funneled corporate assets into a secret budget to pay for a lavish persunal lifestyle, which included throwing these wild parties."

"Everyone looked forward to these parties. They were the highlight of the year. They were wonderful for morale."

"But they must have cost so much."

"For how happy he made us, whatever he paid was an absolute bargain."

"Then we can assume that you've adopted Fezziwig's philosophy and throw extravagant parties for your own employees?" the Spirit said into its microphone.

Scrooge paused a minute. "We prefer to invest in our company's human capital in other ways. We give our employees the chance to pursue whatever is meaningful for them in the celebration sector."

The Spirit asked, "Is that why you only coughed up for a coupon book for Cratchit this year?" Scrooge's face turned red from embarrassment as he stammered, "No comment." He thought to himself that maybe he did owe a little more to the memory of his mentor Fezziwig.

The Spirit pointed to a dark corner of the ballroom and said, "In addition to food and music, it appears the opportunities were endless for sexual harassment as well." He and his crew rushed over, lights blazing, while Scrooge followed in the rear. In that dark corner were a man and a wommon, locked in passionate embrace. Scrooge found it fairly amusing until the couple paused for a breath of air. "Candy!" he shouted.

In an instant the ballroom had disappeared, and Scrooge, the Spirit, and the crew found themselves standing in the back of a dark restaurant. At the table in front of them sat a younger image of Scrooge, as well as the wommon with whom this younger man had just been entwined at the party.

"I thought it would be fun, is all, marrying you," she was saying. "But I was a lot younger five months ago. Emotionally, anyway."

The Spirit asked, "And who's this we're watching?"

"Candy," said Scrooge. "She was my second wife."

The wommon continued. "I never would have gone through with it, had I known you were so divorced from your feelings. You keep me and everyone else at arm's length, then try to double-talk your way out of any real connection."

"Candy, I won't say you're wrong," said the younger Scrooge. "But how many people know themselves well enough to realize that they *are* divorced from their feelings? If I were to admit it, I might even consider this insight a kind of progress."

"Oh!" said Candy incredulously. "Oh! Oh, sure! Oh!"

Suddenly Candy disappeared, and in her place sat another young wommon. "Besides which," this wommon said, "you ought to know I'm not the type of wife who'll smile bravely while her husband holds press conferences to try and clear his name."

"Ahhh!" screamed the genuine Scrooge.

"And who would this be?" asked the Spirit.

"That's Sandy," he replied. "She was my third wife."

"I don't know what you're talking about," said Scrooge's younger image.

"Yeah, right," she said, rather ungraciously. "I know all about the stock split and how you're going to screw those poor coffee farmers."

The younger Scrooge slapped the table. "We're totally within the law on that one!"

"I don't care," she said coolly. "I'm leaving. It's not pleasant watching you sell off your ideals one by one." Then, in an instant, she was gone also, replaced by yet another wommon. The real Scrooge said, without being prompted, "That's Brandy, my fourth wife."

"Fourth?" asked the Spirit. "Guess again."

Scrooge looked panicked. "Fifth?" he asked, not at all sure whether he was correct. And as he stood there watching another set of the angry good-byes at the table, Scrooge's unbelieving eyes were treated to a parade of the womyn in his life. Ex-wives, paramours, common-law wives, sexual surrogates—he got some names wrong, as well as their order of appearance in his life; but they all had the same thing to tell his younger self: He was distant and cold, he worshipped success at the expense of his own integrity, he had used each one for his own selfish purposes, and he would be hearing from their lawyers the next day.

"Spirit, take me home," implored Scrooge. "I can bear this no longer. I can't even keep their names straight."

"But we have more scenes to visit," said the Spirit, "and we have plenty of tape left. What about this union crew? Do you know what this is costing me?"

"No! Take me home! This interview's over!" Scrooge leapt at the camera that had been in his face and tried to grab it from its operator. The Spirit and the rest of the crew wrestled Scrooge away from the equipment, and the melee continued until Scrooge awoke, alone in his bedroom, doing battle with a floor cushion. Sweating and panting heavily, he went to the bathroom, swallowed a couple of Nytol, then staggered back to his mat and immediately fell asleep.

STAVE III: THE SECOND OF THE THREE SPIRITUAL FACILITATORS

crooge next awoke when his watch buzzed the hour. He peered around but saw no spirits to pester him. Yet an eerie light suffused his bed chamber and intimated that he might not be alone. The source of this light seemed to be in his living room, so Scrooge rose from his mat and walked to the door. He opened the door with his breath held fast and peeked in.

What he saw astounded him. Instead of the usual postmodern grays and whites, the room seemed almost on fire with a profusion of warm, yellow light from the Yule log blazing in the hearth. The walls and ceiling were so richly festooned with garlands of holly, mistletoe, evergreen, and ivy that it was as if a rain forest in all its biodiversity had been transplanted there. Heaped up on the floor, to form a type of throne, were geese, game, brawn, great joints of meat, suckling pigs, long strings of sausages, mince pies, plum puddings, barrels of oysters, immense cakes, and steaming bowls of punch—all with enough empty calories and cholesterol to clog the veins of an entire peacekeeping force. At the sight of such an amount of food, the normally temperate Scrooge nearly swooned, half from raven-ousness and half from revulsion. In easy state upon this throne sat a jolly figure of greater-than-average stature, glorious to see, who bore in his hand a glowing torch, which he raised up high to shed light on Scrooge as he came peeping round the door.

"Come in!" exclaimed the Spirit. "Come in and know me better."

Scrooge approached timidly, and asked him not to wave the torch so near to the sprinklers in his ceiling. "Oh, lighten up a little," laughed the visitor. "Look upon me! I am the Ghost of Christmas Present. Let's party!"

Scrooge raised his eyes as he was told. He was relieved to see the warm and jovial look in the Spirit's bearded face. This specter would apparently be less confrontational and insinuating than the last. The Spirit was clothed in a simple yet generously cut green robe that hung loosely on his abundant frame. His dark brown curls were long and free, as free as his unconstrained demeanor and joyful air. Then Scrooge noticed, standing behind the Spirit, another figure, who was more slight and sober in aspect than the other, though not unpleasant. "Who is your companion?" Scrooge asked.

"Oh, him? He's Rupert, my designated driver. Can you believe it? Ha!" The Spirit rose and said, "C'mon, touch my robe. Let's blow this taco stand!" Scrooge did as he was told, and the room and everything in it vanished instantly.

The next moment, they stood in the humble dwelling of a family that existed in a lower percentile of socioeconomic strata. Despite their situation, the family members refused to play the victim, and were chipper and merry in the delights of the season. Love and respect decorated their home as wonderfully as their flocked arboreal companion. The aromas of their dinner lingered welcomingly as the family sat together on the couch, watching *It's a Wonderful Life* on their flickering television. The

Spirit inspected the scene fondly yet intently, then whistled at Rupert and jerked his thumb backward over his shoulder.

Before Scrooge could blink his eyes, he and his companions were transported to a more opulent residence, owned by members of the oppressing class. People were gathered there for an intimate soiree, where they traded confidential and exclusionary information that further secured their privileged positions in society. Food and wine were laid out in abundance, and the guests feasted with little regard for the needs of the workers they exploited. But class warfare was far from their minds this night. The men and womyn were in grand high spirits as they sat around the entertainment center together, watching a laser disc recording of *It's a Wonderful Life*.

Scrooge was struck by the genuine warmth the people displayed for one another while still respecting each other's persunal space. He had not felt such warmth for years, and at this moment was acutely aware of its absence. "Spirit, why do you show me these images?" he finally asked. "Are you trying to show me how isolated I am from my fellow human persuns? How much I have sealed up my heart from the rest of the world? How love is the common link for us all?"

"Nah," said the Spirit from the buffet table a short distance away, "we're just here to raid the 'fridge." He walked back to Scrooge, munching on a large sandwich he had thrown together. The Spirit motioned to the TV. "Y'know, I walk in on people watching this movie just about all night, and I *still* have never seen the ending. Can you believe it? Ha! Let's make like a baby and head out!"

And in the briefest of intervals, the three astral travelers landed in an apartment in the city. It was sparsely furnished yet tidy, and the television had been turned off ("Thank a non-sectarian heaven," thought Scrooge). He could hear voices, a man's and a wommon's, one of which was particularly familiar.

"I don't know," the wommon said, "things just don't feel festive enough to me."

"Do you want to pop the 'Fireplace Log' video in the VCR again?" asked the man.

"Bob Cratchit!" Scrooge blurted out. "Is this his house? And is this Mercedes, the persun with whom he has a primary relationship? My word!"

The Cratchits continued their conversation, unaware of the presence of Scrooge or the Spirits. Mercedes sighed, "No, but it just doesn't feel as joy-ful and exciting these days as when I was a little girl. There are times when I wish I could stop being an

263

atheist, if only for a little while. If only there were more holidays on the calendar for the deistically unencumbered."

From the kitchen came the loud crash of a platter hitting the floor. Scrooge looked in the direction of the noise and saw the big-boned Spirit of Christmas Present emerge, carrying a turkey leg and wearing a comically innocent expression. Roberto ran into the kitchen to investigate. "It must have been the dog," the Spirit suggested, rather speciesistically, as he toddled across the room.

"It must have been the dog," echoed Roberto, who picked up the mess and put the food in the refrigerator.

Scrooge eyed the corpulent spirit with an unmasked disgust. "If you don't have any respect for yourself," he sniffed, "at least try to have some for others."

"Aw, lighten up, man, it's Christmas Eve!" said the Spirit as he alternated bites of turkey leg with fistfuls of Chex party mix. "And the bigger I am, the more of me there is to love. Ha!"

As Roberto walked back into the room, Mercedes said to him, "I think I'm also depressed about how little money is coming in."

"Now, Mercedes," said Roberto comfortingly, "don't fall into the trap of our materialistic culture. We have a roof over our heads, enough food, good friends, a loving child . . ."

"Oh, Roberto, don't talk to me about traps. You're obviously ensnared in a ridiculous 'nobility in poverty' concept that the bourgeois class generates to appease its own guilt. We're not virtuous paupers languishing in some Dickens novel. We've got bills to pay, and that ogre Scrooge refuses to pay you a fair wage."

"I'm trying my best to wreak anarchy at the office," explained Roberto. "I'm striking back at Scrooge in his pocketbook by stealing photocopies and taking too long on coffee breaks. He and the heartless system he represents will come tumbling down before too long." Scrooge was taken aback. He had no idea that Roberto was so bitter, but then again, he rarely talked with his employee about anything in a frank way, and he knew almost nothing of his family life.

"But how does that help us?" asked Mercedes. "How does that help Diminutive Timón? With that huge deductible required by Scrooge's miserable insurance coverage, we'll never be able to afford proper medical care for him."

As if on cue, their vertically challenged pre-adult came into the room. Diminutive Timón was an amiable chap and full of boundless energy. In fact, the only trait that would set him apart from the others in his gender peer group was that his size did not conform to the average. He jumped onto the couch and hugged his caregivers, whose concerns melted away, if only momentarily.

Scrooge's heart was touched by the little pre-adult. He turned and asked, "This boy, Diminutive Timón, what is the matter with him?"

"Nobody knows," Rupert said. "His repeated willfulness and bursts of uncontrollable energy have everyone perplexed. At first it was thought his behavior was a simple case of blocked chakras. But now his condition appears to be a birth-induced delayed trauma disorder."

Scrooge was appalled. "Are there no specialists? Are there no telethons for victims such as he?"

"Don't call him a victim," Rupert said, "he's merely a persun living with a disorder. And telethons, well, they're a little infantilizing, you'd have to admit."

Scrooge thought for a moment, then asked, "Spirit, is his outlook so irretrievably bleak?"

The Spirit of Christmas Present looked him in the face, although his eyes were getting glassy. With bits of food dangling from his beard, he said, "If you'd spring for better coverage, you tightwad, at least they could pay for more tests and treatments."

Properly chastened, Scrooge watched the family play together. How nondysfunctional they were, even with Timón's affliction. Scrooge sadly envied their warmth and their positive, nurturing interaction. After a while Bob announced it was time to toast the season. He got out the glasses and the sparkling mineral water and passed them out to Mercedes and Timón. "A toast," he said, "to this festive season, and may the forces that placed us here (or not) continue to bless us."

Timón raised his glass. "May a higher entity (if there is such a thing) bless us, every one."

They sipped in unison. Then Roberto raised his glass and said, "To Mr. Scrooge . . ."

Mercedes stopped and set down her glass. "Really, Roberto, why spoil our celebration by mentioning him?"

"You didn't let me finish," said Roberto. "To Mr. Scrooge, for so perfectly embodying the enemy of the working class. May he always inspire us to continue the fight!"

Mercedes laughed, and so did Timón. They all raised their glasses and drank. And their laughter and joy continued until the Spirit slurringly announced it was time to move on. As the scene faded, Scrooge continued to stare, and especially kept his eye on Diminutive Timón.

The next sound Scrooge heard (besides the fairly regular moaning of the Spirit of Christmas Present) was the hearty laughter of his nephew. Soon Fred's cozy living room materialized around them, with all his guests who had come there to feast.

"And so Uncle Scrooge just sat there," continued his nephew, "refusing to accept any of my good wishes for the season and swatting away at the bugs on his desk!"

Everyone laughed heartily when picturing the kindness-impaired coffee distributor in such a scene. Until, that is, one persun in the group said icily, "I don't think cruelty to defenseless insects is all that funny."

Fred's countenance changed to a concerned expression. "No, you're right, I'm sorry," he murmured.

The Spirit guffawed and said something disparaging about the group's sexual adequacy, which they were lucky they couldn't hear. In fact, the Spirit laughed so hard at his remark that he lost his balance and stumbled over a footstool with a heavy thump. Scrooge was by now supremely annoyed at the Spirit's loutish behavior. "What's the deal with him?" he asked Rupert finally. "I haven't seen him drink anything."

"It's a substance abuse problem," said the driver. "He thrives on the milk of human kindness, but sometimes he enjoys too much of it."

"You got that right, Rupert buddy," slurred the Spirit as he pulled himself unsteadily to his feet. "And you know the old saying: You can't drink the milk of human kindness; you can only rent it. Excuse me a minute." The Spirit staggered off, looking for relief.

The mood of the celebrants picked up again when Fred's wife announced, "You'll all be happy to know that we managed to dissuade all the local retailers from carrying mistletoe this year. So let's drink a toast to the end of traditionally sanctioned sexual harassment."

They all raised their glasses of non-alcoholic, low-fat, no-cholesterol eggnog, all except one. "Sasha?" Fred asked of this persun. "Is something wrong with the eggnog?"

"You've forgotten," said Sasha quietly. "I'm a vegan."

Fred's face went red. He mumbled numerous apologies and ran into the kitchen to prepare Sasha a beet-juice spritzer. This slight error did not dampen people's spirits long, however, and the festiveness and generosity of the season soon returned. Good cheer and laughter filled the air at the expense of no individual persun or group.

Scrooge got quite caught up in the merrymaking and clapped and cheered gaily at the games and jests the celebrants enjoyed. Fred's guests played at Optically Inconvenienced Persun's Bluff for a good long time, then enjoyed a lively round of Twenty Non-Intrusive Questions. Next they worked at decorating their Yule tree in the most inclusive and equitable way imaginable. Oh! what fun they had, adorning it with Stars of David and menorahs, and oriental dragons and Shinto paper cranes, and stars and crescent moons, and dream catchers of all sizes. They hung holly clusters for the druids, talismans for the Wiccans, and yin-yangs, ankhs, I Ching sticks, Tarot cards, rune stones, and all conceivable manner of symbols and mandalas. When they were finished, the tree stood gloriously and ecumenically arrayed.

Next on the agenda were refreshments, and Fred's guests did eat well. They feasted on salads and casseroles, fruits and nuts, and naturally sweetened pies and cookies until they could find no more room inside themselves. To Scrooge's vexation, the Spirit of Christmas Present could not help remarking disdainfully on the fare, which was too healthful and delicate for his tastes. While he pounded his fists and bellowed that he was starving, the guests heard not a word. Scrooge and the designated driver both noticed how the strong currents of goodwill were causing the Spirit to act very erratically. After the Spirit began to flail about and knocked a platter of baba ganoush on himself, Rupert led him out to the patio where the fresh air would clear his head.

To top off the feast, Fred brought out from the kitchen a steaming platter of low-fat latkes, with generous bowls of apple sauce and yogurt. Although everyone was full to bursting, they couldn't resist gobbling a few of the potato pancakes. As the guests settled down around the living room, Fred brought out a menorah he had purchased just that day and placed a candle in each of the eight holes. He recited what he knew about the Festival of Lights (which admittedly was very little) and lit all eight candles, thus compressing a salute to Hanukkah to fit into their busy evening.

Next Fred brought out a straw mat and placed it under the menorah. "Now it's time for our Kwanzaa celebration," he announced. "You'll please forgive me for using the menorah again, but I didn't have time to find a proper *kinara* at the store." So the guests quickly honored the *Nguzo Saba*, or Seven Principles, while Fred led them in song and mangled the Swahili words he read from his Kwanzaa manual. They then cleared the table for their celebration of Divali, for their guests of the Hindu persuasion. By the time the overstuffed piñatas were brought out for the next phase of the party, Scrooge had walked out to the patio to look for his two astral guides. Out in the cold December air, he spied the Spirit of Christmas Present flat on his back, making hooting noises and laughing at his own private jokes.

"So, where are we off to next?" asked Scrooge.

"Our time with you is almost at an end," Rupert said. "After the Spirit gets this full of the milk of human kindness, any further travel tends to be

counterproductive, not to mention embarrassing."
The Spirit had begun singing "Deck the Halls" loudly, substituting "Fa La La" for all the lyrics he was
forgetting (practically all of them, it turned out).

Scrooge asked hopefully, "Then is my reeducation
over? Have I not been visited by three spirits
tonight?"

Rupert said, "I'm not really a spirit of the season,
just a concerned observer. You still have one more
spirit to meet." Rupert took the hands of the pros-
trate Spirit and began to drag him away. As they left,
the scene changed, and Scrooge found himself
standing in the middle of a cold and lonely plain,
with another specter of gloomy visage walking
toward him out of the murk.

STAVE IV: THE LAST (BUT IN NO WAY LEAST) OF THE SPIRITUAL FACILITATORS

he phantom slowly, gravely, silently approached. When it came near him, Scrooge bent down upon his knee, for in the very air through which this Spirit moved, the wraith seemed to scatter gloom and mystery. For which, of course, we can only blame our own fears and insecurities, which we habitually project onto the unknown.

The Spirit was dressed all in black—scuffed black boots, black leather jacket, baggy black shorts, torn black stockings—with an occasional glint from the studs, chains, hoops, and buckles that adorned the specter's clothing and various bodily parts. Beneath a haystack of bleached and ratted hair, a gaunt, expressionless face was visible, highlighted garishly in mascara and black lipstick. As the Spirit shambled slowly and somewhat absently toward him, Scrooge could not make out the phantom's gender (not that such an unimportant variable would be any reflection on his/her skills or authority). When s/he stepped beside Scrooge, his/her mysterious presence and the smell of tobacco and stale beer filled the man with a solemn dread.

"I am in the presence of the Ghost of Christmas Yet to Come?" said Scrooge.

The Spirit answered not, but coughed, scratched, and pointed onward with a hand.

"You are about to show me shadows of the things that will happen in the time before us," pursued Scrooge. "Is that so, Spirit?"

The Spirit looked at him without emotion, then gave him the quick combination of a shrug, a nod, and a sneer, which Scrooge took to mean assent.

"Ghost of the Future!" he exclaimed. "I fear you more than any other, because I'm a bit of a control freak and dread the idea of looking into the unknown. I felt that I was making real progress with the last Spirit before he became incoherent. Some real growth was happening there. But I know your purpose is to instruct me in the truth, so I place myself in your hands. Lead on."

They walked, but made no apparent progress along the misty ground. Instead, the city seemed to spring up around them and encompass them of its own act. The buildings and byways were familiar to Scrooge immediately. Up ahead in the cold street were a man and a wommon, whom Scrooge recognized as reporters to whom he had often leaked damaging stories about his competitors and other enemies.

"I don't know what he died of," said the first reporter. "All I know is, he's dead."

"It must have been a stake through the heart," joked her companion, "that is, if they could find his heart."

The first reporter sighed, emitting an icy cloud. "He's causing me grief even in the grave. He couldn't have picked a worse time to die. It throws a wrench into the exposé I was wrapping up on his Central American land-holdings. Now I won't be able to confront him with anything on camera."

"Talk to some of the organizers of the farmers' revolt down there," suggested her companion. "You'll get some good video. They're probably dancing in the streets right now."

The reporters laughed at that idea and walked on. Scrooge turned to the Spirit and asked, "Who did they mean, Spirit? What man were they talking about?" The phantom made no reply, but coughed and pointed onward. Scrooge's figure trembled from head to foot as he thought of his nephew's warm, friendly living room. "I'll tell you this at the outset," he informed the Spirit, "I'm not very good with this whole death concept."

Farther down the street, Scrooge and his mal-nourished guide walked up on two men emerging from an office, putting on their overcoats and fastening their scarves against the cold. From the section of town, one could assume their profession most likely was the law. One man told the other, "Without a will, eh? That's going to be some catfight."

"It'll be years in probate," was the reply. "The creditors are one thing, but with an estate that size, those ex-wives will not give up easily."

"They should watch what they ask for," replied the first. "Any stake in that little empire is going to be worth a lot less, once the legal fees come due."

"Well, look at it this way," chortled the second, "he might have avoided paying for our services while alive, but our fair share of his money was bound to come due eventually!" The laughing barristers proceeded down the street, their steps growing ever lighter as they contemplated the great bounty of billable hours.

Scrooge was shaken by their callousness. "I hate to watch a legal mind busy at its ravening work," he told the Spirit. "Parasites, one and all. I might have ruined a few companies and careers in my time, but I never charged a fee for it or pretended I was providing a service."

Because of what he knew of the Spirit's mission, Scrooge tried to find a lesson for himself in all he was witnessing, but the scenes only filled him with dread and revulsion. The relentless silence of the ghostly visitor did not help to soothe him. "Who was this dead man?" he asked. "Is there nothing but cynicism and avarice attached to his demise? Can you not show me something constructive that came of this lost life, or someone for whom his presence and his passing have mattered?"

The Spirit looked at him solemnly, then gave him the same quick shrug-nod-sneer as before. S/he pointed around a corner, and Scrooge proceeded as indicated through the chilly murk. Turning the bend, they found themselves in a wholly new part of town, heading toward a nondescript building whose outsize dimensions were well illumined with spot-lights. Scrooge and his spiritual facilitator drifted past a crowd of patient, shivering people in a line outside the building and melted their way through the cement walls. When they emerged on the other side, they found themselves in the wings of a television studio filled with a live audience. Scrooge recognized it as the set of one of those daytime tabloid talk shows that exploited cheap titillation and personal failures for prodigious ratings. The moderator of the show roamed the audience with a microphone, while her guest for the broadcast sat in a chair onstage.

"And can you share with us what happened after that?" asked the moderator.

"Well, the lack of money in the house always caused tension between my parents," explained the guest, "and all their concerns about my health added to the bad atmosphere there. It was years before my correct diagnosis was revealed, and by that time so much damage had been done to my family that it almost fell apart."

"And tell us, what was your diagnosis?"

"I have acute psycho-environmental allergies," he said bravely, "which means that all the people, all the places, all the objects that make up my surroundings can without warning make my anxiety level go sky-high, and at times give me severe headaches and even a mild rash."

"And you blame your father's employer for all this?"

"Yes, he worked my father to the bone, and provided such shabby health coverage that I went improperly diagnosed for many years."

The host asked, "What was your reaction to the recent news of that man's death?"

The guest sighed. "Relief. I felt justice had been served. Then I felt incredible guilt and anger for my feelings of relief. This man had somehow wormed his way into my mind and wouldn't let go. For all the damage he'd done to me in his life, it still hadn't relented when he was gone. That's why I wrote my book: to purge myself of his influence and make friends with myself again."

"All right, we have to take a break," said the host. "The book is called *My Oppressor, Myself.* We'll be back for more with Timón Cratchit, right after this."

The audience burst into applause on cue, the sound of which caused Scrooge to jump. He stared incredulously at the man on the stage. He certainly looked like Bob Cratchit's son, although no longer diminutive at all. To Scrooge, he looked hale and hearty, in spite of his pious and pitiable expression.

"What is this all about?" he demanded of the Spirit. "How could Timón's fate be tied to mine? I'd never seen him before last night and I expressed enough concern then, even though he merely looked like a regular, rambunctious boy to me. I thought you were here to see to *my* welfare. Why have you shown me this? What am I to do with his whiny revelation?" The Spirit looked at him puzzledly, as if a bit nonplussed at this reaction. It appeared that getting the message through to this mortal would be a bigger challenge than anticipated. The specter paused, apparently weighing its next move, then pointed onward as s/he had so often before.

They passed through the wall of the studio and were suddenly at the gates of a cemetery, where the snow whistled through the twisty weeds that choked the unkept grounds. The Spirit stood among the graves, coughing and pointing down to one headstone. Scrooge was disoriented and shivering. His pulse began to race as he sensed his journey with the phantom was drawing to a disturbing close.

"Why have we come here?" he asked. "I've already told you, I don't deal with these kinds of things well."

The Spirit again pointed at the stone, beckoning the man to read it. "I know intellectually that this is all part of the great cycle of life," Scrooge explained, "but I have a real problem with it emotionally. And you, Spirit, have become a very depressing companion. All these cheap theatrics aren't doing me much good at all. Ask of me anything else, but please don't make me read the stone."

The Spirit was immoveable as ever. Scrooge crept forward, trembling as he went. He pushed aside the weeds and read the stone of the neglected grave, upon which was carved his own name, EBENEZER SCROOGE.

"No, Spirit, no!" he cried. "Now you've gone too far. The other spirits worked my emotions over well enough. Now you come along to intimidate me with all these scenarios and alleged conversations, only to bring me here to confront me with my own mortality! I've never heard of such flagrant entrapment!"

Scrooge angrily dusted the snow from his hands and began to rise to his feet. "You and your pals ought to look at yourselves in the mirror before coming around to improve other people's characters. All this manipulation, all this sordid play-acting! On top of all the insults and indignities that have been heaped on me tonight, you decide to show me that I may die! Well, forget it! Enough is enough! I reject it, and I reject you!"

The Spirit's eyes were wide with amazement. This was indeed a first in his/her sepulchral experience: a man confronted with his own inevitable demise, who attests that for himself it is merely an option.

"Take me back to that TV show," said Scrooge, "and I'll show that little crybaby Timón something. I'll show him the pressures of owning a business and employing subversive ingrates like his father." Scrooge approached the Spirit menacingly. The Spirit, eyes wide and darting back and forth, took a few steps in retreat. "Take me back to those reporters and I'll show them what bunch of leeches and lemmings they are. They want to confront me on camera—I'll give 'em some good video."

Scrooge now had the Spirit's arm and was holding fast, while the phantom, at a total loss, began struggling to get away. "Take me to them all! I'll tell that bunch of whiners where to get off! They expect the business owner to have all the answers and solve all their problems, then they despise him for their own helplessness! They don't know what I go through! I deserve better treatment than this!"

And as they wrestled, Scrooge saw the Spirit go through a transformation. The hair shrank, the body went limp, and Scrooge found himself wrestling with an oversize arrangement of dried flowers.

STAVE V:
THE END OF EVERYTHING

es! And the dried flower arrangement was his own. The sleeping mat was his own, the halogen lamp was his own. Best of all, the time before him was his own, to plan his revenge in!

"It's over! I am done!" said Scrooge in relief. "The Spirits have finished their work, all in one night! And Jacob Marley, take heed: They did not beat me!"

Scrooge sprang from his mat and paced the room, inspecting everything there to make certain he was awake. All the while, he continued to talk to himself: "What nerve, rubbing images of possible mortality in my face. They *all* had their nerve, trying to make me feel guilty! Ha! If anything, they showed me that I'm the product of my environment! All the pressures put on white males! It's no wonder I am the way I am! It's not my fault at all!"

He charged out into the living room, not even pausing to put his clothes on properly. He was too excited, too indignant, too ready to act on what the Spirits had shown him. "Thanks, Jacob! You sent the ghosts here, that I might discover what's real and true! And I found out the truth about what I'd imagined all along: Everyone's against me and blames me for their problems. So who's the real victim here? Me! That's who!"

These revelations sent Scrooge into giddy fits. He made many plans for his day, and for the near future. "I'll start a radio show to address the abused and underappreciated white males in this country," he said to the empty room. "No, a cable network. No, better still—I'll run for office, to protect the interests of white males and businessmen everywhere! Whoop! Ha ha!" And Scrooge laughed at himself and his agitation, a laugh that would certainly chill anyone who heard it.

Without even pausing for his usual gruel-pancake breakfast, Scrooge left his condo hurriedly—there was so much he had to do! He had to fire Bob Cratchit for his pilfering and sponging! He had to draw up a will, and leave each of his ex-wives a big goose egg! He had so many things to do, but first he had to get to his office. Where was his Volvo?

"Ah me, I'm so giddy and excited, I must have walked right past it! Ha ha!" Scrooge retraced his steps in the small parking lot then spun round again. He knew exactly where he'd parked it the night before, but now that space was utterly vacant. "What! Where?" screamed an incredulous Scrooge. "Where is it? Who'd want to steal a nineteen-year-old Volvo?!"

Infuriated, he was about to storm back inside to phone the police when yet another bright light flashed before him and left him visually nonreceptive for the moment. When he recovered, he saw in front of him what must have been another spirit, yet the appearance of this one was the most mundane and ordinary of any he had seen (not that there isn't some magick to be found in the mundane and ordinary).

There before him stood what appeared to be a middle-aged wommon in a navy-blue polyester suit that lagged severely behind the fashion curve. She wore her hair up in a pile that was slightly askew, and her glasses were perched at the end of her nose and fixed around her neck on a chain. In her hand was a metal clipboard, which she perused. She had about her an air of complete indifference. On the lapel of her jacket she wore a plastic pin to celebrate the season, a cute Saint Nicholas that moved like a jumping jack (or jill) when its little string was pulled.

"Mr. Scrooge?" she asked, without looking up from her clipboard. "Ebenezer Scrooge?"

"That is I," he said, somewhat testily. "What do you want of me? I'm in a terrible rush."

"I'm sure you are," she said emotionlessly. She flipped a few pages, then looked up. "I'm here to offer an official apology for all that happened last night. It was something of a mix-up."

Scrooge couldn't believe his ears. "What? Who are you? How do you know of last night?"

"I am the Supervisory Spirit of Intercessory Therapeutics," the specter said. "I'm in charge of coordinating the caseload of all the spiritual facilitators that are working to help persuns change for the better at this time of year. I sent the Spirits to you last night, as well as Rupert the driver. But my orders were somewhat garbled when I received them, and I'm afraid you were subjected to the wrong therapy last night."

Scrooge's mouth hung open. Even with every-thing he'd been through, such a thunderbolt he never expected! He felt his anger begin to rise. "What do you mean, 'wrong therapy'? How could such a thing be?"

"We do our best, but mistakes do happen."

"What about Marley? He—"

"It's no use blaming any particular shade. You must understand, we reeducate thousands of per-suns every day, and we're especially busy at this time of year. You yourself must realize how hard it is to get work done during the holidays."

"Meddling, incompetent spiritual bureaucracies!" groused Scrooge.

"I apologize for any inconvenience," the Super-visor said, officiously and insincerely, "but this is for your own good and everyone else's. According to your psychological profile, Mr. Scrooge, last night's method of therapy would be of no help to you, and might even reinforce your negative traits. I'm afraid this may have already happened. However, there are other treatments."

"What other treatments?" demanded Scrooge. "I'll not allow—"

"There is Past Regression–Future Progres-sion, which you had last night. For the severely despondent, we have Negative Alternative Outcome treatment, which we in the profession refer to as a 'George Bailey' session. But for you, Mr. Scrooge, we have something much more direct and traumatic. But it is for your own good, trust me."

"What do you mean, 'traumatic'?" he asked. "Last night was no walk in the park."

"Your treatment plan calls for Rapid Materialistic Voidance," the Supervisor explained. "In it, you will be deprived of all the worldly attachments on which you place so much importance. In order to improve your character, we are forced to ruin your business. To start with, a government report is going to be released tomorrow, showing a definitive link between coffee drinking and liver disease. The price of your stock will plummet, and all your stockholders, including yourself, will take a tremendous loss."

Scrooge looked panicked. "No! Wait a moment! I have to get to my warehouse!"

"You needn't bother. It's already in flames and quite beyond salvage."

This second blow sent Scrooge reeling. The work of a lifetime, up in flames—and he'd decided to let his insurance lapse just last week! "This is too much," he said in a shaky voice. "I need a drink of water. Let me go inside a minute."

"Oh, I almost forgot," the Supervisor said. From her pocket she took a small remote-control box, fumbled to turn it the proper side up, then punched a large red button with her thumb. Heavens, the ear-splitting sound! A fierce, fiery explosion blew out the windows of Scrooge's apartment, scattering debris and broken glass throughout the courtyard. "There. You are now on the road to recovery. Congratulations."

Scrooge sank to the ground and sat on the pavement. His ruin was indeed complete. He looked up at the Supervisor, broken, stunned, near lifeless. He moaned, as much to himself as to the phantom, "Now what, now what?"

"Believe me, Mr. Scrooge," said the Supervisor in sincerity, "we know what we're doing in our department, our little scheduling snafus aside. You'll recover from these setbacks with a greater understanding of what is of value in this world, and what is not."

"I have nothing left!" he shouted. "What is there of value for me now?"

"There is one thing," she reminded him, "although I am speaking quite apart from my official capacity right now. You still have the invitation to your nephew's house. I suggest you take him up on it and soak up some of his hospitality. Play some Scattergories, maybe watch the Grinch on television. You need to reconnect with the persuns around you, and Fred's would be a good place to start. It's been a pleasure serving you, Mr. Scrooge, and again, I apologize about last night." The Supervisory Spirit put her clipboard under her arm and without apparent effort receded into the background and disappeared.

So, with no other course of action apparent to him, Scrooge did as the Supervisory Spirit advised. He managed to hitch a ride from a truck driver hauling a load of frozen turkeys, and within a short time he was knocking on his nephew's front door. And he tried to enjoy himself with Fred and his wife, although the taste of "humble pie" was new and not wholly agreeable to him.

Over time, Scrooge worked hard to learn the lessons that his misfortunes were supposed to teach him, and in the end he succeeded. As he worked to rebuild his company, he learned the value of friendship and cooperation (mainly the friendship of bankers and industry insiders who helped him get back on his feet). He learned the value of giving, especially to the politicians who would protect his interests. And he learned that he was not alone in the world, and so paid more attention to his public image.

Finally, as a result of the intercession of the spiritual facilitators, Scrooge made certain to follow the exact letter of their teachings (if not their true intent) as it served him best, for he was fearful of undergoing more spiritual therapy or traveling with the ill-bred Ghost of Christmas Present ever again.